# Sometimes
# After Dark

J Dark

Published by Paper Angel Press
paperangelpress.com

ISBN 978-1-949139-37-2 (Trade Paperback)

10 9 8 7 6 5 4 3 2 1

FIRST EDITION

## Dedication

*To all those who have gone before,*
*those who are with us,*
*and those to come.*

## Acknowledgements

*Any book requires a team to make it from a dream to a manuscript to a book on a shelf. Paper Angel Press did that for me, and I am ever grateful for that. It's a tremendous labor of love and I cannot thank them enough for believing in this project.*

*I want to thank everyone who has read a book also. You people who love to read are why books are made. Thank you so much.*

# CONTENTS

# HOT DROP

*This story came about from my desire to try my hand at a straight science-fiction story. It went well until one line changed the whole direction of the story. That I hadn't planned on this happening made me want to see where the story wanted to go. It pretty much wrote itself from that point on.*

# HOT DROP

THE HATCHWAY DOOR SWUNG OPEN, slamming with a hollow clang against the bulkhead. The lanky Sergeant Vinson, in full combat gear, woke the team. His raspy drawl sounded like a bandsaw cutting metal.

"Y'all be gettin' up! Control's got us'ns a mission ta go! Report fer briefin' in five!"

"Yes, Sergeant!" The six-unit team shouted as they scrambled out of their bunks and stumbled to their lockers.

Corporal Tripoli watched the others beginning their daily kit up. Grabbing the door of her locker, she lifted its latch. Its door swung open, revealing her gray jumpsuit uniform, fittable armor plates, and wrap-around torso armor with its air-tight helmet. She pulled her helmet on and checked the seals. Satisfied, she removed the helmet and hung it back on its peg.

Next, she grabbed her jumpsuit and zipped in. She finished kitting up, then pulled the helmet back out of the locker, hanging it on a belt loop before hurrying after the others to the briefing.

The briefing room aboard the *Erie* was a small alcove set along inside bulkhead of the bridge. At the center of the floor, a small holotable was already active. There was just enough room for the troopers to squeeze around it.

Lieutenant Kestrel waved his hand over the table, then gestured upward. A blue and green sphere rose from it, stopping to hover at eye level, spinning slowly. Normally, there would be more colors on the map, depicting terrain features like deserts and mountain ranges. Here, there was only green and blue, vegetation and water. The unrelieved green was confusing, as if the data was incomplete.

"You'll note," the Lieutenant said firmly, "that there's only two forms of terrain: forest, and water." He paused a moment. "The forest consists of the same vegetation throughout its reach; the screen isn't broken. Every piece of land above water is covered by vegetation."

The ethereal orb continued to rotate, showing the distributions of land and water. A single yellow spot blinked on the southernmost landmass. Kestrel clicked a button. The hologram flattened and zoomed in dizzyingly to reveal rugged terrain and the outline of a three-building complex. Seven red spots appeared on the screen.

"This is your objective." A red dot appeared south of the objective. Kestrel continued, "This is your insertion point. They'll know you're coming. We can't get into position in stealth mode because of the defense screen. You will make a low-orbit drop by rocket-assist capsule, and deploy at three hundred meters above the ground." He paused, scanning the alert faces around the table. "The landing's going to be rough; I won't lie. You're going to have minimal time to control the drop. Blip the brakes fast, get to ground, and off enemy radar."

Kestrel frowned, then continued. "We don't know what kind of anti-air defenses are deployed. One thing's certain: with a defense screen that sophisticated out here, this place is going to have equally sophisticated weaponry to repel attacks. Keep your heads low, listen to your squad leaders … and Take. That. Objective. Get the job done, and come home. Good luck. Prepare for drop."

"YESSIR!"

The team jogged in formation to drop fitting. The suits they wore consisted of a series of exoskeletons that surrounded the operator. Armor was eventually added, contoured to roughly fit a humanoid outline. The armor bulged around the active frame, making the suit appear vaguely gorilla-like, with large, thick arms and legs in contrast to the relatively thin torso that housed the trooper. Each suit was modified according to the wearer from the standard design.

Vinson led the team past Wendell's suit, which towered over them. He was the heavy support. The suit was reinforced, its skeleton laminated to handle the auto-cannon's recoil. Wendell's armor was easily a head taller than all the others, reaching three and a half meters. Wendell himself was about as opposite as possible from the imposing suit he operated. Quiet and almost invisible, even in groups, he never stood out, even with his eye-catching two-meter height.

Marco's suit was next. His suit was heavily customized. The tiger-striped black and brown wasn't regulation, but Marco was very good, and Command cut him some slack as the pattern wasn't neon orange and yellow, like a previous time. Vinson shook his head. He'd never met anyone who wanted attention like Marco. The man would wear a clown suit on a battlefield. Despite the extreme extroversion, Marco *was* a team player *par excellence*. He'd never pulled anything that threatened unit integrity while on-mission. Off-mission was another matter, and not something the sergeant worried about.

As Marco dropped out of line to suit up, he passed the smallest suit. Barely the minimum one-point-seven meters tall, Carter's suit seemed even smaller cradling the Mk-951 assault weapon. Carter had passed as "Expert" in the weapon, and was a sniper-quality marksman. He was, like his suit, small, intense, and focused. Just slightly over a meter and a half tall, pale-skinned and very lean, he appeared almost emaciated. He'd shaved his head and lathered down with chemical epilators so that his suit contacts and feedback had no hair that might cause even a blip of resistance. Vinson wondered at this, as the sensors had no trouble with hair, but Carter had insisted. Carter's quirks weren't troublesome to the team on mission, so Vinson let it slide.

The next suit had curves no man could fit into. This was Tripoli, Vinson's assistant squad leader. Like her namesake, she was dark-haired, brown-eyed, and olive-skinned. She also stood just over a meter and a half tall, and could handle a Mk-951 like a kid's plastic toy. Like the others, she had her quirks, but those quirks had kept her and others in her squad alive. Her focus on mission was laser tight. It made her a good number two, but Vinson didn't think she'd make squad leader until she got more flexible in her thinking. Like the others, her ability to hyper-focus was both a weakness and a strength.

Last came Simon. His suit was so regulation that it seemed out of order. It was the only suit the sergeant had ever seen that did not have some kind of modification. It matched its wearer to a "T". Of the team, Simon was the most laconic out of mission. He was also the most even-tempered in mission as well. His laid-back demeanor was nearly alien to Vinson and the others. Vinson hated his attitude, but loved his skills. Simon himself was just a shade over one and a half meters, and massed one hundred thirty kilograms. Stocky, but with unbelievable endurance, he was the team's medical specialist. His skills were called upon when the armor could not control a wound — which was, fortunately, not often.

Vinson marched to his suit and saluted it. It had earned that respect from him. His suit looked battered, and almost slovenly, but Vinson wouldn't have it look any other way. Each hole was patched, but not cleaned and smoothed. The dents from shrapnel were left untouched, just the paint replaced. Each time he looked at the suit, he counted each mortal wound it had saved him from. To date, the count was twenty-seven; he'd be dead that many times without it. He dropped the heartfelt salute, stepped onto the small platform, did a precise about-face, and stepped backward into the suit, which started through the automatic button-up sequence.

Once sealed and cycled, the team marched down the gantry to the drop chutes. Vinson had them count off by numbers and step to each opening. The platforms dropped them to loading, where their armor activated, drawing the soldiers up into fetal positions, then enclosed each of them in a gleaming, finned egg.

The ship bucked as it skimmed the top of the atmosphere. Readouts in the capsules reported their oxygen use, blood energy, and administered drugs to ease those whose heart rates went above the physiological optimum.

Weapons reported ready, and the spatial coordinates fed into the capsules, aiming them at their targets. Wendell, the auto-cannon support member, began to hum off-key. The tune was picked up by Simon, who, unlike Wendell, had an ear for music.

The two dissonant warbles grated on Tripoli's nerves. "Shut up or there's gonna be friendly fire!" she growled into the comm.

"Easy Corp," said Wendell. "We'll take it private."

Two light pops indicated that the two men had left the channel to private A, just as an extra strong buffet gave notice that the drop units were unshackled and primed for launch. There was barely enough time for the troopers to take a breath when the rockets engaged and the seals popped, using the air in the tube as the propelling charge. The fins shifted, jinking the capsule in random directions to throw off any enemy targeting. The troopers didn't feel the ride, as neural white noise was fed into their nervous systems, essentially putting them into a state of total sensory deprivation.

The missiles jinked again, and then accelerated toward the surface. Their outside surface temperature climbed to eleven hundred degrees Celsius from the atmospheric friction. After thirty seconds of no hostile response, the capsules straightened their trajectory, and powered down toward the target zone.

Two long minutes passed for Lieutenant Kestrel as he watched the individual capsules streak toward the ground. The systems reported optimum zones for all of his charges. Smiling grimly as his men dropped, he activated the link, then sent a test pulse to check for any jamming. When he got the signal back, Kestrel boosted the signal and set the scrambler to active. The computer would analyze the jamming and look for weaker signal strength to punch through, or open frequencies to operate within the white noise. On the ground, the same kind of electronic war was being waged, trying to identify the intruders, and estimating their landing trajectories.

The neural link dropped. Marco awoke immediately, the warning pings of capsule breakup were sounding, readying him to blip the boot jets to start arresting his fall. He had enough extra fuel for twenty seconds of burn; three seconds would halt a terminal dive. His computer was giving him a choice of controlled burn, fast drop, or manual.

He blinked at the manual control on his HUD, then yelled "Hands in the air, riders!", before laughing with the adrenalin rush and blipping his boot jets.

Kestrel saw Carter, Vinson, and Marco drop computer control for manual, and smiled for a moment. "You wreck those suits, you Yahoos, you're doing latrine duty for the next twenty years."

His eyes were drawn to the screens as the boat's optics detected movement on the ground at the base. "Our hosts are rolling out a hot welcome. No heavy weapons identified, yet. Twelve count, no armor. IR says the weapons are warm, lasers or plasma tech, most likely. We've got twenty laser bursts, should you need 'em."

"Loud and clear, mother hen," Tripoli said over the comm. "You get a call if we need you to lay an egg."

A couple of muffled laughs came over the comm. The lieutenant smiled then said, "Ten seconds to touchdown, you're armed, weapons hot, HUD link on. Hoooah!"

"HOOAH!"

The capsules burst, their pieces darting away under power, broadcasting random signals to draw fire away from the dropping marines.

＊    ＊    ＊

The drop went totally uncontested. No anti-drop fire. No missiles. Nothing. As the squad dropped, boot jets fired asymmetrically in programmed jinks and jukes, creating random shifts in direction and speed to foil targeting. They dropped into the trees. Its canopy swallowed them, forcing the light compensators to adjust rapidly, making the interior of their helmets seem to flicker. Once down, the drones were launched, two per squaddie. Each drone fed data of the surrounding terrain, heat signatures, air samples, and medical information to the orbiting mother ship. The drones, about the size and shape of a thumb, skittered back and forth on small, motor-less fans set at their corners, allowing them to hover silently and change direction in an eye blink. The drones swiftly dispersed, according to squaddie tactical assignment.

The humidity measured at ninety percent, with the atmospheric temperature a sweltering 40 degrees Celsius. The leaves overhead were so thick, light barely penetrated to the forest floor. On the ground, the closest thing Vinson could compare the visibility to was a deep twilight. All the trunks and branches seemed to almost melt into one another in the near-darkness.

Rotting vegetation covered with the forest floor. Nothing grew the first six meters up; there just wasn't enough sunlight. The middle canopy was a ten-meter-thick crazy quilt of moss, dead branches, and vines. The top canopy was about four meters thick, with entwined branches sprouting what looked like leaves of every shape and color imaginable.

The highest leaves were every shade of green, with brighter hues lower into the canopy. Green gave way to yellows, then oranges and reds as the light dimmed. Under the suits' lights, blue feathery things shared space with orange clusters and reddish branches that seemed to create a net at the base of the upper sections. The light breeze that moved the upper leaves seemed to transmit its way down to the lower areas, where even the small patches of moss swayed in time with the upper branches, but there was no measureable wind to move them.

Most striking, the sergeant noted, was the absence of noise: no buzzing insects, no wildlife calls — just the quiet rustling of leaves overhead, and the soft, woody creak of swaying branches. The silence was so encompassing that it seemed press down and cover everything like a shroud.

The marines unlimbered their pulse rifles and swiftly moved to assigned locations. Alert and ready for a fight, they dug in, their armored hands tearing scars in the earth to lie down in. Entrenched and camouflaged, they waited for the enemy counterattack they knew was coming.

"You think they're gonna come on the ground or in the trees, Wendy?" Carter whispered over the comm.

"Twenty cred on a ground attack," replied Wendell, with a muffled grunt that might have been a laugh.

"Shut. The. Hell. Up." said Vinson. The authority in his southern drawl cut through all chatter, leaving the channel dead. "Attention squad one-two-two, you have movement your direction. Mother counts seven — confirm seven — with contact. One-two click, twice to acknowledge."

Simon keyed his mic twice, the double click registered by the ship. The code made hacked communications more difficult. Calling the member number with the request made it hard for the hacker to duplicate quickly.

"Team two, you're up that ridge, low on our side. Make sure you all got good cover," Vinson ordered.

"On it," Tripoli replied. "Marco, you're point. Wendell, you're drag. Move out."

Marco grunted over the comm, then sent his two drones ahead to sweep for hostiles and map terrain. Tripoli did the same directly over the team, with Wendell running sweep circuits at the rear.

Vinson gestured to Simon. "Simon, over left, Carter, over right. I'll be point man first. We use hand signals here on out. Make sure you can give cover fire if a squaddie needs it."

"Sahmon, oveah thar, Cartah, over thar. A'll be up front fuhst. Use hand signals heah on out. Make shor ya got cover fiah for us'n if we need it."

Both men nodded and melted into the dark, their combat armor displayed matching background patterns as they moved, rendering them nearly invisible to human eyes.

Vinson thought for a moment, then dialed up the low light option for his armor. As dark as this place was, there'd likely be some sharp eyes in the forest. He checked the ammo counter on the clip, then brushed his hand across his web-belt, making certain everything was in place. His fingers touched the small, sewn-on snap pouch just to the left of the buckle, hapatics in the suit letting him feel the small imperfections in its stitching. The pouch wasn't regulation, but, for him, was his strongest reason for service. His fingers stroked the pouch tenderly, then dropped to the pistol grip of the pulse rifle. He bent his arm overhead, straightened it twice, and then started working slowly along the ridge.

The going was rapid., With little undergrowth to traverse, they moved the first five kilometers quickly. The drones kept reporting no movement, no local wildlife. The last was very unusual. Every place had some kind of indigenous life.

Tripoli and her team checked in visually, making certain no one was drifting out of formation as they paralleled Vinson's team. Everything they saw was the same: absolutely no animal life of any kind, the branches and leaves moving as if pushed by a light breeze. All of the instruments in their suits recorded no air movement strong enough to account for their motion. The wet ground muffled their steps, making their reconnaissance absolutely silent, except for the odd moment when a suit would brush against a trunk or a low-hanging branch. It created an eerie, unsettling feeling as the team approached the structure that the lieutenant had highlighted.

"Hell! What happened to my drones?!" Carter's voice cut across the comm like a knife.

"SHET UP, CARTER!" Vinson roared.

Marco checked his drones "vitals". They all showed green, then nothing. Simon watched the same thing happen. No red blinking lights for a malfunction, no beeping indicating a target lock on the drone. Just there, then gone.

Vinson guessed the drones were being taken out by their yet-unseen enemy. Just how they were doing it, was the question. The last of the drones winked out, leaving them dependent on their own suits and senses.

Using hand signals, Vinson slowed the squad's approach. Moving slower was the only tactic to deal with the loss of the drones. They still hadn't seen anything of their supposed enemy after the first contact back on the ship. The six marines moved carefully over the top of the ridge, and then partway down the sunward side. The objective of the recon and rescue lay before them.

The structure was massive. Vinson pulled out his binoculars and dialed back the power to fit it all within his sight picture, then keyed the binoculars to measure the distance. Data flashed across the display:

RANGE:1.411KM WIDTH: 2.103 KM HEIGHT: .608KM

Vinson pulled the binoculars down.

*Christamighty, it's huge. The trees must be twice, three times the size of what we've seen so far. Where are the hostiles the ship showed us? This place is dead quiet.*

Vinson raised his hand, then clenched it twice. The two fire teams hunkered down and set up covering fire.

\*     \*     \*

Simon moved into a small clearing, away from the cover of the trees. He unlimbered his entrenching tool and rapidly dug a shallow pit to lie in. He didn't know why, but being near those softly swaying branches sent shivers up his spine. A few moments later, he was in the trench with his rifle propped up on a small berm of soil. From his position, he could easily cover Vinson's path along the edge of the structure.

*The sooner I'm offa this rock, the better. Place reminds me of a cemetery; nothing but breeze in the leaves. Wonder where all the wildlife is? A place like this ought to have at least some kind of local bugs.*

He shook his head then lowered his eye to the 'scope once more.

Vinson continued his slow traverse along the edge of the vegetation. He watched the Sarge for a few more paces, then swept ahead and behind, looking for any movement. When he swept back to check Vinson, he saw the Sarge step behind some brush. He never came out.

Simon waited for a few moments, then swept his scope back and forth, checking for any movement. He scanned the opposite slope, ground, everything, three times before he decided to move out toward the Sarge's last visible position. He hand-signaled the corporal, then crept forward, fighting his revulsion as he stuck to the darkest, densest cover he could find. Slowly, he picked his way down slope toward the last location where he had seen the sergeant.

"Private Simon, do you have eyes on Sergeant Vinson? We've lost telemetry from the squad leader. Signals are flatline." After the enforced silence, the corporal's voice sounded like an explosion in his ear. Simon dropped to one knee, looking about carefully from his limited vantage point in the huge trees. There was nothing — only the slightly swaying leaves and branches that they had trekked through. He tapped his comm twice for a negative reply.

"This is Lieutenant Harris. Corporal Tripoli, until Sergeant Vincent's status is ascertained, you are acting squad leader. Radio silence is hereby revoked. Members, call in by the numbers."

"One-two. One-three. Two-one. Two-two. Two-three," the members called in.

"We copy, sir. Permission to speak, sir?" Tripoli said.

"Granted," Harris agreed.

"Why break silence now?" Tripoli asked bluntly.

She looked around at the others, and saw the same question in their eyes. Breaking comm silence was not something the team did, or the commander did, during ops. This change in operations surprised everyone.

"Your team is compromised, Corporal. Sergeant Vinson disappeared without a trace. What is your assessment of your situation? Is operational silence going to be any advantage?"

Tripoli considered this for a moment. "No. If the Sarge's been taken by locals, silence isn't going to help us. They'll have been tracking us for a while to take Vinson so fast."

"Command agrees. If we had not been observing operational silence, we may have had warning, and been able to direct you beforehand," Harris said. "We still need the structure scouted. That is your first priority. Second is Sergeant Vinson. Mark his last known location. Recon and return here. Command will scan from here and see if we can locate the sergeant. Questions, Corporal?"

"None, sir. Repeating orders: recon structure, find sergeant Vincent, rendezvous after recon this location."

"Correct. Move out, and good luck."

Tripoli looked at the team. "You heard Command. We've got recon to do."

"Yes, Corporal," they said in unison.

"One team, Simon, you're point. Wendell, you're drag. Carter, you're moving with Simon. Marco with Wendell. We go bounding overwatch. We're going to move one and a half klicks North, then turn and go in from the Northwest. This place is big; don't get confused by the size. Gear on. Simon, you and Carter are go."

*        *        *

Tripoli watched the two marines moved North. They ran three seconds hard, then dropped, rolling in opposite directions, stopping when they were behind cover. She nodded to Wendell, and he and Marco moved out, with Tripoli dropping next to Simon. She watched them rush past Simon and Carter, then run a good twenty meters past, and then drop, rolling and seeking cover. Then she was up with Simon and Carter, stopping next to Wendell as they rushed up.

They kept up the grueling pace for the next thirty minutes, each team advancing by ten to twenty meters. No one said anything, alert for any motion not their own. Their movements were fast, compact, running low to avoid stirring any branches, their feet picking up cleanly to avoid shuffling and noise. Each fall, controlled, being a half-roll to deaden the impact and present the most difficult moving target. With all the care and attention they paid, only the stuttering sounds of their own footfalls could be heard. The absolute silence wore on Tripoli; she knew it wore on the others, too.

*What kind of place is this?* Tripoli wondered silently, growing more concerned about the Sarge's disappearance.

When her inertial compass reported that they'd moved a half-kilometer past the north edge of the huge edifice, she called a halt. All of the marines were breathing hard, almost exhausted by their pace and actions.

"Water and food, no fire, make it fast. The hard part comes next," she told her team.

As they ate and rested up, she moved to the crest of the ridge and tried to look down at the structure through the trees. She knew where the structure was, according to the downloaded map in her wrist comp, but it proved impossible to see from her vantage point.

*We'll take it slower now, and a lot tighter.*

Tripoli watched the huge trees in the distance sway rhythmically back and forth. Even with her external laser microphones turned up as sensitive as possible, there was no sound. No wind. No creak of swaying trees. Only total silence – except for her team's voices and her own breathing. The silence felt ominous, and somehow alive. Her thoughts made her shiver.

*Why can't I shake this feeling? It's like we're whistling in a cemetery.*

"Command, reporting no hostiles. What happened to the seven signals during the drop?" she inquired.

The silence over the comm seemed to stretch out for minutes.

"We don't know," Command finally replied.

"What do you mean, you don't know, sir?" Tripoli demanded, seething inwardly.

*How can you not KNOW what happened to seven hostiles? We had satellites launched. We have full coverage of the area! How did you fucking LOSE seven hostiles?*

"Control's best guess is stealth technology. We're working that angle, and hope to re-establish contact soon." There was a pause, then Command said, "Parameters remain the same. You have a schedule to keep, Corporal. We will keep you updated."

"Yes, sir," Tripoli replied crisply. The channel popped as it as it closed. Then she screamed in rage, "Updated, hell! You find them! I'm tired of being led by the nose in a place that doesn't have anything we're looking for, and you damn well haven't said anything about this 'science expedition' that we're supposed to find! What in HELL are we doing here?"

\*       \*       \*

She made certain the channel remained private. Sealing herself in, and turning her ECM systems fully active, she raged at their nebulous orders. It was clear to her that the entire mission had been a misdirection of some kind, but for her life she couldn't figure out why. There seemed to be no reason for the sudden capriciousness of their orders. As she raged inwardly, it felt like a fog was lifting. Her head started to ache, then cleared.

*What the hell is happening?*

She remembered the mission. They'd been tasked with a rescue, to be certain, but it was a rescue of the rescue team and the original science team.

"Our last mission was a complete failure. Something affected the team through the power suits. There was no communication and the radio chatter, while sounding normal, was not the parameters that had been in the briefing. Keep alert and observe two changes in standard operational procedures. One, always remain in visual range of each other. Do not use your HUD; use your eyes. Two, maintain constant communications with Control. Keep the comm open at all times. Do not go dark."

*We blew it! What is going on here? How did … the ECM gear. I turned it on to keep from being heard by Control.*

Tripoli looked at the others, all of whom had settled down on the damp earth. Their bodies had turned toward her, waiting for orders.

She moved to the nearest soldier, and pressed her helmet to his. "Wendell, can you hear me?"

"Shore can, Corp."

"Turn on your ECM, then get Marco to turn his on."

"Done." Wendell's hands came up to his helmet. "Oh man!" He started to pull at his helmet, then stopped.

Tripoli kept her helmet tight against his. "Wendell, you good?"

"Frosty, Corp. What is that? My gawd, what they hell was hap'nin to us?"

"Get over to Marco, and get him on ECM. I'll get Simon and Carter."

A few minutes later, all five had their ECM on and were discussing the situation. They huddled close, five helmets in a circle pressed tight to one another, so their voices could be heard.

"We call for pickup, and get this intel back to Control," Marco said.

"No. In order to call for pickup, we have to drop the ECM, and we don't know how fast this operates. For all we know, it could be instant," Tripoli said tersely.

"They gotta know something's up. Going dark was what they specifically said not to do," Simon replied, remembering their orders.

"Good sense," Tripoli replied. "But the wrong choice here. ECM's the only thing that cleared our heads."

"I wonder why it works," Simon asked thoughtfully.

"Right now, I don't care. It's got our heads clear, so we keep them going and see about the Sarge first, then the mission," Tripoli said. "You apes ready to go?"

"Locked and loaded!" came four muffled voices.

"Good. Simon, Carter. First team, you lead out. We go a slow walk. Watch for movement or noise. Use hand signals. If you see something, call huddle."

"Yes, Corp," both Simon and Carter replied.

"Move out." Tripoli told them.

✳    ✳    ✳

Now that their minds were clear again, the soldiers noticed much more around them. The forest seemed alive, watching them as they backtracked to Vincent's last location. They found him within ten feet of his last transponder location. His suit was partly covered with what appeared to be roots. His armor had been etched and weakened by what seemed to be a viscous acid seeping from the roots. The team converged to pull at the roots and try to tear them away from the sergeant. Wendell checked Vincent's armor over carefully, while Simon checked his bio readings.

"The etching's bad. Another hour or so, and the roots would have breached the armor," Wendell informed Tripoli. "It's barely airtight right now. He needs repairs."

"He needs emergency evac, and we can't do it," Tripoli replied. "Simon, can you get the suit to pump him with stimulants? We need him alert."

"I don't think it's gonna help, Corp. These readings say he's in a coma. The stimulants will just boost his heart, not wake him," Simon said. "He needs a full medical."

Tripoli growled in frustration. She looked around at the faces in the helmets. Her command. Her responsibility.

"Simon, you carry the Sarge. I'll take point. We go slow. Move out."

*       *       *

The team moved slowly back down into the bowl. The silence they first encountered was still absolute, but now the movement of the plants felt all had more ominous. Grass, brush, and tree limbs all seemed to stretch toward them as they passed. Everyone in the team seemed disturbed by this, Tripoli observed. The helmets would turn and focus on each movement until the troopers stepped past it, and then their helmets would swivel to the next large movement.

Simon was especially agitated as he tried to make certain he was facing the threat. Sarge was his responsibility, and nothing was going to get to his charge while he lived. The trees continued to grow larger as they descended to the bottom of the bowl, becoming as big around as some of the pictures of the extinct sequoias on Earth. To look at them was to feel dwarfed by their magnitude.

They moved slowly toward the stone structure. Compared to the ancient solidity of the trees, the buildings seemed an aberration. No visible impressions of their age were immediately apparent. Their surface seemed fresh and new. Up close, Tripoli couldn't see any visible lines where blocks nestled against each other to form the walls of the structure. The wall itself was forty meters tall, and stretched for a half-kilometer. Its single doorway looked like a small mouse hole by comparison.

The team moved into position, with Carter and Wendell flanking the doorway. Tripoli waved them over, and the team again leaned into a huddle, helmets touching.

"It's the only place we can go, and I already hate it," she told them. "Carter, you're point. Wendell, you're drag. We're likely gonna be single file in there. Simon's in the middle. I'll be behind Carter. Marco will be behind Simon. Keep the jammers going and keep your eyes open." She checked her chronometer. "Thirty seconds to check weapons, then we go."

"Yes, Corporal!" came the reply.

Carter took two deep breaths, clicked on his helmet light, and then the camera. He rolled around the corner, his weapon raised. The light beaming from his helmet showed a narrow corridor going straight for at least eighty meters, which was the limit of its range. He switched to infrared to see if there was a difference and, when no detail emerged, returned to standard light.

The five marines slowly moved down the narrow, cramped corridor. Compared to outside, this was nowhere near as threatening. Close-quarters and house-to-house combat they were trained for; for a silent, enigmatic forest that seemed alive, they weren't.

Ten minutes later, the corridor expanded into a large cavern. As they moved into the immense space, the air seemed to begin to glow with pale bluish-green light. A few more steps into the cavern brought the light up to a normal daylight level.

The place was enormous. The ceiling registered on sonic ranging as two hundred meters overhead. The room measured as three hundred meters across, and nearly the same wide. A soft material covered the floor. The database reported it to be a fungus.

The five marines had moved together to huddle and discuss options, when Vincent went into cardiac arrest. His suit began beeping loudly. Simon rolled the sergeant onto his back and plugged into its emergency override circuit. Rapidly, he scanned the physiological readings, which were all red-lined.

Vincent's heart was pushing two hundred forty beats a minute; oxygen saturation was down to a bare minimum. Blood pressure, even with the high heart rate, was barely eighty over fifty, and sinking fast. Diagnostics indicated critical nerve damage. Simon looked on in helpless agony as Sarge's heart suddenly seized, and then stilled.

Tripoli leaned her helmet against Simon's. "How bad is he?"

"Gone, he's gone. We can't even suspend him. There's no way the suit could take the temperature, damaged like it is."

Even as he spoke, Simon was keying the emergency cryogenic response in Vincent's suit. The system began to hum. Micro-lasers fired, cooling the suit, and Vincent's body, for cryogenic suspension. The suit beeped a warning as stress on it increased from the temperature gradient. There came a slight groaning sound, then the weakened ceramic gave way with a sharp crack, crumbling into pieces. The laser array shorted as the electrical storage discharged with a loud pop and a bright blue spark.

"You tried," Tripoli said, with forced, focused calm. "Wrap him and set him by the tunnel. We'll pick him up on the way out."

The group was somber as they wrapped the sergeant in an environmental blanket. A quick spray of adhesive sealed the covering. Once the sergeant's remains were positioned by the door, Tripoli called them all to a huddle.

"Whatever's going on, we're seeing this through. Sarge would want it that way. Simon, you're point. Wendell, you're second. Marco, drag. Carter, behind me. Whatever's down here is what we're after, and we're gonna get it." Tripoli paused, then said sharply. "Move out!"

"Yes, Corp!"

∗    ∗    ∗

The team shouldered their weapons, and started slowly across the floor in single file. Each marine was careful to follow the foot prints of the squaddie in front, hoping to avoid any weaknesses or traps hidden in the soft fungus floor. Simon slowly worked his way across the cavern, angling left, toward the only other opening he could see. As they approached the archway, it became clear that this was an artificially enlarged passage. The corridor was much too clean, much too regular, to be natural.

*This is the real deal now,* thought Tripoli.

She checked her safety by flicking it on and off, making certain her weapon was ready. The others checked their weapons. This change meant that the mission was on now. With a heightened sense of purpose, the small group pushed forward down the corridor.

The darkness began to fade as they moved down the narrow passageway. Light seemed to come from all around them: the floor, walls, and ceiling.

*I wonder if it's piezoelectric?* Simon mused.

He increased his pace slightly to move ahead of the others a few extra meters. The others widened the gap between themselves also, taking the cue from Simon. If any blast happened, spreading out lessened the chance of all of them getting taken out at once.

The light continued to increase as they moved, becoming so bright that the soldiers had to deploy their sun filters to see at all. Tripoli tapped Wendell on the shoulder, then motioned for him to tap Simon and stop. She wanted to see if the light would fade when they quit moving.

Tripoli motioned them over and got them in a helmet-to-helmet huddle once more.

"What we have is a lotta light from somewhere." She checked her readouts, which irritatingly showed no unusual energy or magnetic readings.

*This is really giving me a bad feeling. There should be some kind of energy spike to get light like this, but the suit's sensors say nothing's there.*

She gritted her teeth for a moment, then took a deep breath to calm herself before speaking again. "I think it might be from us, charging something as we walk. We're going to take a fifteen-minute break to see if the light dissipates." She looked around the huddle at the darkened helmets.

"What if it don't?" asked someone.

*Carter,* Tripoli thought from the accent. "Then we improvise," she replied, "and keep going. This is the only path, so it's the only way the science team and the other rescue parties could have gone."

"What do you think the others did with the light?" another muffled voice asked.

"Probably the same we're gonna do: live with it … if we have to," Tripoli said as an answer. She didn't like the idea of going into the light.

The glaring brightness held its intensity for five minutes, then began to fade slowly. As the soldiers waited for the light to weaken completely, they re-checked their weapons, re-checked their suits, and re-checked their ECM gear, making certain everything was ready.

It took another fifteen minutes for the light to disappear entirely. Oddly, their suits didn't register any brightness change. Tripoli had to manually flip on her helmet light on in order to see.

*I wonder if they waited like that?*, Tripoli asked herself.

Units like hers were trained for aggressive action and, usually, any obstacle was met and dealt with through improvisation. "Be a smart marine. Figure it out on the fly," Vincent had told them time and again during practice. Tripoli thought about the words, and wondered about the first rescue team.

*I don't think they did slow down for the light. It might have done them.*

Her helmet light revealed the long narrow corridor once more. As they moved down the passageway, the floor was barely illuminated with a faint-bluish green tinge. Tripoli took point this time, checking her weapon to find it charged and the safety off. She carried it low in both hands. Each step had her swiveling her head forward, up, left, and right, checking everything in front of her for any hints of traps or irregularities in the floor or walls.

The light slowly strengthened again as they pressed forward. This time, it increased to a particular level and stayed there, right near normal daylight. The effect was somewhat disorienting, as the light radiated from underfoot.

Another ten minutes brought them to another widening in the tunnel. The huge, nearly spherical cavern stretched for nearly eight hundred meters across, according to Tripoli's ranging optics. The narrow footpath angled down into the depressed center, where a large nest of strange objects sat. The entire area covered by the objects stretched two hundred meters across the floor of the sphere, creating a maze the team would have to travel through to get to the other side.

Simon kneeled at the sharp edge of the bowl and ran a finger along its smooth surface. "We don't want to go that way. It feels like it's greased."

"Define 'greased', Simon," Wendell asked him.

"We get a free ride to the bottom. I don't know if we could stand up once we got there. My fingers couldn't get the slightest grip when I tried to check how smooth it is," Simon reported quietly.

Tripoli looked at the faintly-lit path angling down to the machines. She motioned the team to huddle and touch helmets again.

"Stay on the path, weapons hot. That looks like too good a place for an ambush," she growled at them.

"Yes, Corp!"

"Look for anything that might give us a clue where that first rescue team and the scientists are. Rescue is first priority, after staying alive to do it."

"Yes, Corp!"

"I've got lead. Wendell, you're number two. Simon, you've got rear. Carter, you've got left; Marco right. Six meters between. We can't jump off the path, so keep the distance."

She straightened up without waiting for the reply, checked the ammo counter on her rifle, then started slowly down the narrow walkway. Once she'd gone seven steps, Wendell moved onto the path, his weapon aimed down, ready to fire, his finger resting lightly across the trigger guard. Each member started seven steps behind the previous squaddie, with Simon following last.

Their sense of proportion seemed all out of place once they started in. The "towers" seemed to enlarge oddly as the team moved closer, looming over the marines like antediluvian monsters of stone. Strange machinery spun and blinked as they stepped to the edge of the first tower. Tripoli's range finder reported the distance across its base as three hundred meters. Perplexed, she measured the range again and got the same result.

"How can the bowl be eight hundred across, and just one of these things be three hundred alone?" she muttered to herself.

Tripoli checked to make certain her suit was sealed. A strange reading like this might mean she was falling under the influence of whatever was in the atmosphere again. When the integrity check showed a green light, she shouldered her weapon and slowly moved in between the weird objects.

Gravity here fluctuated constantly. One moment, the pull would be normal. Then, in the distance of a few steps, it would swing, and the team would find itself angling up to twenty degrees from vertical, forcing the marines to gyrate wildly to stay upright. Another few steps, and they'd stagger under twice the pull what they were used to, then a few steps later, scrambling frantically as they suddenly weighed a fifth of what they should have.

As they progressed through the bowl, random pieces of machinery started to hum softly, beginning to move and shift, changing in size and shape. Their perception skewed as the machines sped up their movement. Everything seemed to lose its sharp edges. Things blended together, flowing into, and around, one another. Simon saw his weapon's barrel twist like a live snake trying to escape his grip. Marco and Wendell seemed to flow into one being with dozens of small identical faces on the end of thin stalks, then the hand-shaped body broke in two, and re-formed back into Wendell and Marco once more.

The team struggled forward, starting up out of the bowl. Tripoli focused on the far arch, doing her best to ignore the wildly variable environment around them. Carter failed first. Tripoli turned as he tore his helmet off and howled madly, clawing at his armor as it seemed to liquefy and spin around him. He screamed like a lost child, falling to a fetal position and sublimating away.

Wendell died next, screaming and laughing like a madman as his auto-cannon spewed snow and fire. The cannon exploded, covering him in some liquid-like acid. He was still laughing as he melted away, his voice echoing faintly for some moments afterward.

Marco's armor collapsed as he seemed to deflate within it. The baggy armor and clothing struggled to hold its shape for a few seconds, then dropped flat on the ground, dissolving into a greenish mist that was slowly drawn into the whirling machinery.

Odd shapes and lights clattered, sped up, then gave a screech that drove ice shards into Tripoli's mind. Both her and Simon covered their ears, and struggled to stay upright, fighting for balance against the vertigo.

*Sarge is gone, I have to make it. I owe it to Sarge ...*

Tripoli watched Simon pull himself painfully back together, and stumble a few steps more. Something ripped at her insides like broken glass. She gritted her teeth as her body tried to blow itself apart, holding her mind together through sheer stubbornness.

She took one step, then another, and another, staggering, barely upright as she fought forward. This was not about rescue any more. It was pure survival. She glanced to her right, and spotted Simon moving toward her. His movements were like an old man's, tentative and slow, fearful that he might fall apart with each step.

She raised her hand, gritting her teeth in pain. Simon's hand rose toward her. His face was skeletal, glistening threads of blood dripping from it. Their hands met, and Tripoli felt an electric charge tear through her. She dropped to her knees, gasping, still holding Simon's hand. His face was normal. His slightly off-center eyes gazed back at her in dazed recognition.

Simon got his feet under him, rising, his hand still wrapped around hers. She willed her legs to move. It was as if she hovered just outside of her body, unable to feel it, yet manipulating it, like pulling strings on a marionette.

They stumbled forward, then released each other's hands. Immediately, the wrenching feeling of being consumed returned. In his blind flailing, as he doubled over in pain, Simon struck Tripoli's arm. The sensation stopped as they made contact, leaving them both in a cold sweat inside their suits. Tripoli looked at Simon's grip on her arm, then at his face. He looked as shocky and pale as she felt, and guessed she didn't look any better to him. She wondered again if her suit had been compromised. If it was, then Simon's was also. She looked his suit over carefully for rips or punctures, and was relieved to find none.

"Come on, Private. Get your lazy ass up," she said with a pained gasp. "We got to finish this and get out. Command's got to know what happened."

She didn't wait for an answer, dragging the stocky medic to his feet. They both began to stumble through the machinery, slowly heading toward the bright aperture in the side of the mountain. Why they both thought this way was "out", wasn't questioned. It was the fastest way away from the painful, terrible machines.

The two of them staggered onward, toward the opening. Their steps became heavier, as if the world itself tried to crush them flat against it. Whimpering as they bogged down, Tripoli tried one last resort, and triggered her adrenalin dispenser. She felt the nozzle press against the large vein on her inner arm, and the high-pressure pump fired the concentrated liquid into her blood.

In moments, her heart rate tripled and everything slowed around her. The liquid had been added to the suits as a way to combat the shock of grievous wounds, giving a soldier a chance to survive, or spend their remaining life covering their team members. She reached over to her wrist comp, and triggered Simon's adrenalin pump remotely. Their steps steadied, though the terrible weight didn't recede. They reached the opening, and plunged through it. The light swallowed them whole.

Tripoli tightened her grip on his arm. She could barely make out the path through the blinding light. The path angled upwards suddenly, nearly causing them to lose their balance. She half-dragged him forward, covering front and left, as he tried to cover right and to the rear.

The light started to fade as they pushed on. Dim outlines that looked like large, twisted pillars that reminded Simon of the trees they'd first traveled through. His heart pounded from the adrenalin. Each footstep sounded like a gunshot, even muffled as they were through his helmet. His feet finally caught up with Tripoli's insistent tugging, and the two began to jog forward, double-timing their movement.

\*　　　\*　　　\*

The ground began to crackle, like dry twigs rubbing against each other. Simon looked down, then focused his eyes forward, cold sweat forming anew across his brow as he realized they were jogging across bones. There were so many skeletons that the ground beneath them couldn't be seen.

The blue-green light vanished as they passed through a second archway. It opened into a clearing where the ground was bare rock with a translucent, brownish look to it. In the center of the clearing, lay the remains of six bodies. Simon knew who they were without looking at the ID tags. He knew the bulky outlines of Wendell and Carter. He recognized Vinson's lanky form lying next to Marco. There two more, their hands clasped together: himself, and Tripoli.

Tripoli dropped to the ground next to her own body. The adrenalin was wearing off, leaving her completely exhausted, unable to react to the scene in front of her. She was too tired to scream.

Simon collapsed next to her as his own adrenalin stimulation wore off. He kept staring at the two bodies with their hands intertwined.

"That's ... us?" he asked Tripoli.

"I don't know," she replied tiredly, then her voice hardened. "No, that's not us. It's just an illusion this crappy place is doing to us. It's like the stupid illusions before we went full seal! They're not real!"

She lurched to her feet, and screamed in incoherent rage.

"THEY. ARE. NOT. REAL!"

The plant roots shot from the ground, entangling them both. Tripoli was pulled under, struggling against their grip, still screaming. The plants arrowed toward Simon, then seemed to pause, as if waiting. He stared back, fear gnawing his stomach raw.

"I ... I'm ...", he started, then began to cough, sobbing raggedly. "I didn't want to die ... I didn't ... I ... oh god ..."

The plants ignored him, drawing back down into the ground. The clearing faded as another arch appeared.

"I didn't wanna die," he sobbed as his feet impelled him through the grey gate, then he disappeared.

Tripoli watched him fade, and a raw scream of rage and despair ripped from her throat as the vines finished dragging her into the ground. Her vision faded to black …

\*       \*       \*

The hatchway door swung open, slamming with a hollow clang against the bulkhead. The lanky Sergeant Vinson in full combat gear woke the team. His raspy drawl sounded like a bandsaw cutting metal.

"Y'all be gettin' up! Control's got us'ns a mission ta go! Report fer briefin' in five!"

"Yes, Sergeant!"

The five-unit team shouted as they scrambled out of their bunks, and stumbled to their lockers.

Corporal Tripoli watched the others beginning their daily kit up. Grabbing the door of her locker, she lifted its latch. She paused and looked at her hand. There had been the faintest sensation that someone's hand had held hers for a moment. Turning away from her locker, she looked at the rest of the team, then shrugged.

She finished kitting up, then pulled her helmet out of her locker, hanging it on a belt loop before hurrying after the others to the briefing.

# THE DAY

*This story was written due to a request for submission and, while it was too short for the publisher, it works just fine here.*

# THE DAY

TODAY WAS THE DAY. It was simple to beat security: walk up to the unit before the detail was there in the morning, slide the pistol on the table past the detector, and step through. Easy-peasy. Then it was just jamming the pistol back in his jacket pocket. With the heating being totally inadequate in the back room, it'd be natural to wear a heavy coat while loading the trucks.

It wasn't something planned; it just happened because of yesterday. Yesterday had been hell. Everyone screaming to have their packages done first. Everyone else screaming for supplies, for change for their cash drawer, for a break. The only one to do it was him, and he couldn't keep up with all of it. Everyone got mad and yelled. They all yelled at him because of how slow stuff was.

Well, he was through being the whipping boy that everyone took stuff out on. He was going to show them all just how powerful he really was, and they were all going to pay! He'd give them exactly what they gave him: hell with no mercy. All the yelling, all the insults, all the hate. He'd share it with them all, and laugh as their faces exploded. His revenge would be complete.

He patted the pocket with the pistol. It lay in his pocket like a gavel on a judge's desk, ready and waiting to pronounce judgment. And they all would be judged and found wanting as human beings. He couldn't wait to see their faces. See all the fear — the realization that he was life, or death, for all of them.

With these happy thoughts racing through his head, he began the day of sorting and setting up the stations. Some of the early shift had started filtering in to find him, like usual, here early and already working. There were a couple grumbles of "brown-noser", but he smiled like he always did, and mentally filed away the faces for extra-special treatment when the fun would start.

He kept at his job: keeping the clerks stocked, moving boxes, clearing trash, smiling all the while … and imagining how spectacular their faces would splash when the bullet hit them Right Between The Eyes. *Yeah buddy, that will be so sick, it'll be awesome.* He could paint the walls red, baby! Total red!

The thought excited him, making his hand itch for the handle of his Colt .45 automatic. He stored the extra clips on a web belt with enough carry to hold an even dozen. He planned on using them all. How many times had he been belittled when he was even the tiniest bit late? How many times had he been yelled at because he was working too fast?

How many times … the insults and screams and abuse filled and filled him like a water hose filling a balloon. As soon as the balloon stretched too far, the water burst it. He felt that way: like one more little thing would explode him if he took any more crap from those assholes.

He spent his entire lunch break at the corner table, furthest from the door. The sick-looking grey-green tile and dull tan walls that always reminded him of fresh vomit didn't even create a twitch in his gut, so absorbed was he in the petty abuses he'd suffered.

*One more,* he promised himself. *I'll only take one more. Then I'll kill 'em all.*

He left his hamburger untouched, along with his drink and fries. He was locked in — a hand-grenade with the pin pulled. The first jiggle and bye-bye boom. He was so ready.

He returned to his job, smiling, thinking of the moment, THE moment. It didn't happen in the first hour after lunch, then it didn't happen over the second hour, then it didn't happen over his afternoon break.

He was grinding with impatience, and nothing HAPPENED. It was enough to drive him crazy, and when he realized what he had told himself, he burst out giggling. Old Bill Crupky, the head postmaster, poked his shaggy gray head in.

"Something funny, Johnson?"

"Uh, no sir. Just a thought hit me funny." He almost made himself laugh again.

Krupky nodded, his gray ponytail swinging behind the lion's mane of shaggy hair. "Come to my office. We need to talk."

This was it. His mind leaped with unholy glee. THIS WAS IT! The "one more". He'd burn them all down! Kill them and set the place on fire! No. Beating them to death with the wrenches in the back! No. Shooting them in the guts to hear them cry! His head swirled with the things he'd do. Oh, the things he'd do! He was more than ready!

He followed Krupky into the postmaster office. The dingy ivory walls were like those in the lounge. Despite his excitement, some little part of him still quailed at the thought of committing murder. That little voice was lost behind the burning crazy train of gleeful rage that tightened his muscles, preparing to swallow him whole.

He waited impatiently for Krupcky to settle into his ancient-looking recliner. Its battered brown leather creaked as Krupcky sat down. Krupcky steepled his fingers in front of him, then took a deep breath.

"Johnson, I wanted to tell you …" Krupky stopped talking as he opened a drawer on the blonde wood desk. Johnson could hear papers moving.

*He was going to get fired! That would be it! The last straw! THE LAST F\*\*\*ING STRAW!*

His placid-looking smile widened into what he thought might be a death grin. That thought set off another fit of near giggles.

He managed to keep them silent as Krupky pulled out an official-looking manila envelope. He checked the front of the envelope, then handed it to Johnson.

"Open it."

Johnson gleefully tore it open, looking for the pink slip of doom. What fell out instead was a white, folded piece of paper, didn't look anything like a termination notice.

His gleeful bloodthirst stumbled in the reins as his whole being ground to a screeching train wreck, resonating *"Huh? WTF is this?"* throughout his body.

`Dear Mr. James Jesse Johnson:`

… was how the letter began. It looked so official Johnson about choked on the sudden lapse of bloody anticipation. He read on in growing disbelief …

`Your manager, Mr. Prentiss Krupky has submitted on your behalf, and we have approved a one`

```
dollar per hour raise in your salary, backdated
to your anniversary period. The difference will
appear in your next paycheck.
```

All thoughts of revenge and mayhem fled, squealing in terror at the astonished joy and triumph that burned forth like a glowing sun. He didn't know how to handle the news. A direct lightning hit couldn't have shocked him more.

*A raise! A backdated raise! With extra money!*

He only heard Krupky's voice as a dull buzzing as he floated six inches above the battered polyester cord cushion of the chair.

He remembered to shake the Postmaster's hand as he floated out the door and down to the locker room, and pulled out his murder bag and carried it over to the maintenance closet. A chair and some enthusiastic shoving pushed the bag out of sight on the top shelf where nothing was ever put.

He stepped down and moved the chair back to the pink, vinyl-topped table, then closed the closet door ... and his mind to the thought of mayhem.

*A dollar and hour raise! And backdated pay! This was a time to celebrate!*

At quitting time, he hopped in his car, then drove directly over to his sister's and took her out to a wonderful lobster dinner with all the trimmings. He giddily paid in cash, and spent the time during the meal to tell her what had happened. She was ecstatic for him and said so. He dropped her back at her place, then drove home and slept soundly for the first time in months.

He was back at work the next day, smiling and pushing carts full of boxes, and re-stocking the clerk stations. Their snide comments and teasing rolled off him. He found that knowing he was worth an extra dollar an hour made it easy to talk back a little. He had found his footing in the office, pulled his head together.

The days rolled into weeks, and weeks into months. He became less standoffish, more assertive, and, with those changes, more approachable. He rose through the ranks, eventually becoming postmaster for the office, holding the job for fifteen years.

All the while, the murder bag gathered dust and remained forgotten … for the most part. After work on rough days, Johnson would pull out the stepladder and climb up to view the bag, gazing at it for an hour or so, and wonder "What if?". Then, he'd put the ladder back, go home, and ready himself for the next day.

And, on days when he was feeling nostalgic, he would sit as his small wooden desk, open the middle drawer, and pull out a faded letter that began:

Dear Mr. James Jesse Johnson:

# SAYING GOODBYE

*This story is another deeply personal one that came about after a friend passed suddenly away. It percolated for a while, then burst forth. This one went ninety percent complete about two days after I started it. It consumed me up to the point where the main character drives out to Big Bend Park. Despite only taking a few days to nearly complete, this is one I had to walk away from often, to calm down and let the story out. It was a series of manic spurts and periods of time away to let the emotions settle enough to start writing again. It was a catharsis for me; I purged a lot of grief and anger in the words.*

# PART ONE

*Live — Lightning Crashes*

D O YOU KNOW HOW YOU'RE GOING TO SAY GOODBYE to someone? Is it going to be a loving embrace and a soft caress of their cheek before they go to the great beyond? Or, is it going to be heated words and a pistol stuck in their belly as they try to argue, or to plead with you, not to pull the trigger? Or is it simply a call in the night? A quick stop at the mortuary to look at a lump of flesh bloated with formaldehyde, because that's the law? Or, will you, like me, wonder what happened when they just disappear? Here one day, and gone the next, and no clue where.

I remember — or think I do — the last time I saw Mom and Dad. They'd dropped me off at Uncle Soap's apartment after packing the beat-up gold Ford Taurus for a camping trip.

They often went camping alone at least twice a month — down in the Big Bend National Park. I remember Dad wearing his red-and-black-checked shirt he'd pulled the sleeves off. Mom always told him that was her favorite shirt of his. She'd wear it around the house sometimes to tease Dad. Not that they were all sweetness and love. More than once I heard them screaming back and forth about all sorts of things. Almost always it was about drugs.

I didn't understand then, but I think I do now.

They argued the most just before they went camping, and were best together after they got back. As a child, I saw the change, and knew it had something to do with them going camping, but it really didn't matter. Mom and Dad were happy. They paid attention to me, and bought me things like a new set of shoes, or a cool shirt. It's funny that I remember the clothes, but not their faces. I remember Dad always being skinny, and he had fuzz on his face. I don't remember if it was a beard or mustache, both, or if he just didn't shave every day. Mom was like Dad — skinny.

When they didn't go camping, Dad stayed home nights with me while Mom went to work. She'd always dress up in baggy pants and a shirt, and carry lots of bright, flashy clothes that fit in a little carry bag to work. Dad would stay awake with me until I got tired, then I'd get tucked into bed on the couch at the far end of the trailer. I'd fall asleep listening to Dad watch television.

Every so often, before I passed out, I'd watch him give himself a shot of 'medicine' in between his toes. I know he was shooting up now, but then I knew he was always more happy afterwards, so it seemed a good thing to me. I knew something was off — most four-year-olds can sense things. We're not yet aware enough of how to lie to ourselves and avoid uncomfortable truths. Denial and delusion aren't something that's learned right away.

Mom dressed all the time in old clothes and dark colors. When we went out to the store, it was usually in the very early morning. Mom always told me that it was best, because there weren't many people around, and it made shopping easier. Looking back, I think it was because at those hours, hardly anyone she had met at her 'job' would be around. She table-danced, or stripped — whichever describes it best for you.

Mom hated it, and came home crying a lot. That would make Dad unhappy and those were when the biggest fights happened. About her job. About the money she brought home because dad couldn't work. About him not working. They always fought about that. They didn't pay much attention to me then. I learned to hide in my room when their voices started to get an edge. It meant that things were going to get broken, and a lot of slapping and throwing. It was better in my bedroom.

As I look at the memory of it, that room was my refuge — the one place I had some little privacy of my own. It wasn't sacrosanct. Both mom and dad would come in to wake me up, or yell at some accident, or even hide from one another, either in play or … you know. The not-fun-not-play stuff like fighting or yelling or crying. Dad did it a little more than mom. He'd charge in and slam the door, then lean against it. Mom would pound a few times, then go quiet. Dad watched me as he leaned on the door. He'd hold his first finger to his lips and go *"shhhh"*.

I took the hint and leaned silently against the door with him. I barely came to his waist as I pushed to hold the door closed. Dad grinned lopsidedly at me. Mom would pound on the door until she got tired, then go into their room and lock the door. Then dad would open my door, and go back to watching TV, or make some crummy sandwich from whatever was in the fridge.

Other times, it was mom who ran into the room. She'd lock the door like dad, then push my bed against the door. My bed being the futon mom and dad got for me to lay on. One side smelled like smoke and vomit, making me want to throw up too. If I turned it over, then it smelled moldy. I snuck a blanket into my room and put that on top of the moldy side. I wasn't moldy then, just damp and moldy smelling.

Mom, toward that last day I saw them, began taking medicine earlier and more often. She needed it, she said, because the management said that the dancers ("entertainers", mom said) had to show customers a real good time if they got asked. Mom said she didn't like it because it made her feel icky all over, and the medicine made the icky not bother her so much.

In crude adult language, mom was supposed to go have sex with men who paid the manager for the privilege. That's what I found out later. I knew mom felt bad whenever she had to be 'friendly'. She'd come home, throw her purse and dancer's bag on the floor, then run into the bathroom and throw up in the toilet.

Dad would get upset that mom was sick. He'd yell that she should stop working that 'shirthole' of a place. Mom said he couldn't get a job, so she had to work there. They would start arguing about everything. I would go to bed, falling asleep to the shouts. I would wake up in the morning and hold my tummy because I knew they were unhappy. It was like the moldy spot on the futon: mom and dad felt moldy. Dad started taking medicine a lot more too. He would drink until he giggled, then get the needle medicine and stick it in his toe. He bit down on a sock or a pencil because that hurt more.

It was then that the scary man came to the house. Mom and dad looked scared when he showed up. They sent me into my room. He watched me walk all the way to the door. I knew this because I watched him; I looked back over my shoulder all the way. He scared me so much that I didn't want to turn my back to him. His eyes reminded me of the monsters dad giggled at when he was drinking. The red eyes scared me more than anything. I kept waking up thinking he was in the room with me. Mom and dad didn't like that, and I had to stand outside on the front stoop until they let me back in after the sun came up.

But, despite all the troubles, I felt loved. My parents paid attention to me. Not always kind and friendly — they sometimes punished me for things I didn't understand — but they gave me attention all the time. At the age I was, attention was always welcome, even if pain was part of it. Mom and Dad were gods. They fed me, housed me, and, on occasion, actually loved me. It was a place I knew I belonged. The troubles went away after the scary man came.

Mom and Dad started going out camping together. Both came back happy. Both gave me attention that made me happy. It was exciting. Neither of them were fighting any more. The bad old days had disappeared with the visit by the scary man. I got things. Toys. Clothes. Not just new clothes, but new clothes so stiff they itched me. They had funny tags on them. The food was sweeter, and there was more of everything.

# PART TWO

## *Candlebox — Far Behind*

MOM AND DAD WOULD GO OUT CAMPING a lot over the next year, according to Uncle Soap. He would take care of me while they were away on the weekends. Uncle Soap was a short, round man with white wisps of hair making him look like the character from the Back to the Future cartoons, only not quite as tall or skinny. He was always talking to himself. All day long he would mutter about rain, about warming, about trash overload, and people overload. I think he was a researcher of some kind.

His apartment was more cluttered than mom and dad's — only it was paper. Paper was everywhere. Newspapers stacked nearest the door. Sometimes they would be a whole stack; other days almost nothing. In the small living room, there were so many stacks of paper that it was a maze. Uncle Soap had paths to the TV, to the kitchen, to his old yellow sofa he slept on, to the bathroom, to the faded blue easy chair with a brown stain where I threw up when I was sick once, and to a locked door at the very back of the house that he never opened while I was there with him.

Uncle Soap was a good man. I liked going to see him. He was never cross or angry at me, and he never hit me about anything. He answered any questions I had about anything. He always watched out for me. The attention was so much that it was like he was smothering me on some days. I'd go hide in the small square of empty space just behind the faded blue easy chair, and look at the newspapers, imagining tall white buildings that things went on in: a person making a stamp, and stamping out comics.

The back window was actually a sliding glass door. It had stacks of paper all the way across the bottom that were as tall as my chin when I looked out. The old brown curtains reminded me of mom and dad's linoleum floor back home. I could part the curtains and look out into a cement back yard with a strip of ground that was an amazing green color. All the grass in that strip was the same height, and a lush texture that didn't look at all like the ground around mom and dad's trailer.

The ground around the trailer was brown, mostly. Small single plants poked up out of the dirt here and there, looking like grasping hands to me. I didn't like the yard, and stayed inside when I could. Mom and dad would make me go outside when they wanted quiet time. Everything around the trailer, and the other broken-down trailers, made me think of animals crawling off to die.

Which is what trailer parks remind me of whenever I drive by one. They're not dead-ends for broken dreams; there are many families that do well. It's my own memories that create the image that I see whenever I pass by one. The trailer park we lived in, the *Western Spur*, was truly the last refuge of broken dreams and wasted lives.

I didn't like it, but children can adapt, and I was able to make some friends, or make up others when the few other kids like me weren't around. Being the youngest meant that I was always the last one to be able to do anything if I was in a group. That was, I think, what made me value time alone. I didn't have to wait, and I didn't have to do what the bigger kids wanted to. I could go at my own pace, explore what interested me, and not what someone else decided was the thing to go do.

It was kind of how mom and dad were after the scary man came by. They quit seeing friends, except for Uncle Soap, and kept the curtains pulled so there wasn't any way to look outside. They still put me out to play, but it wasn't the same. Most of the other kids had moved away, or were now in school, so there was no one to play with, and I wasn't enrolled in kindergarten. So that meant I spent most of my home time alone outdoors.

My days were being pushed outside when my parents woke up, being given money to go to the little general store at the entrance of the park, buy a snack for lunch, and then stay outside until the afternoon, when mom and dad let me back in to play in the house, eat dinner, watch TV, and then go to sleep, to do it all over again the next day.

This went on, until the day that next spring. Mom and dad dropped me off at Uncle Soap's. I don't know if it's me looking back and trying to put some prescient thought into that day in my mind, or I did actually pick up that my parents were more excited than usual for a camping weekend.

I remember them dropping me off the usual way, by honking the horn on the old gold Ford Taurus, and waiting for Uncle Soap to walk out. Once he waved at them, mom shifted the car in drive, dad yelled, "G'bye kid! See you Sunday!", and turned up the radio. With music blaring from the car, mom drove out of the parking lot, turned right, and disappeared behind the red brick wall at the entrance to the apartment complex. That was the last time I saw them.

When they did not show up Sunday night, Uncle Soap became worried. He paced more than usual. He talked to himself and walked over to the pink-colored telephone on the stack of papers nearest the kitchen entrance. He picked the receiver up, then tapped away at it. He growled into the mouthpiece, then listened intently. His face flushed red and he looked more like a mad scientist as he picked up the body of the phone, pacing in agitation back and forth in the little kitchen. He screamed at the other person, then slammed the handle back down on the body, and, with exaggerated care, placed it back on the stack of papers.

That was the first night without my parents. I stayed awake all night waiting to hear the familiar mutter of the car's engine, and mom beeping the horn. It never happened. I wasn't worried. I did recognize the change in routine, but being with Uncle Soap made the unusual situation bearable. Uncle Soap was really good at putting me at ease. That sense of comfort dissolved with the next angry phone call to whomever he was talking to. His yelling was louder than mom and dad, so I hid in the stacks of papers until he stopped yelling.

The days began to set a rhythm: early morning breakfast of cereal and bacon, lunch of a processed meat and cheese, and dinner consisting of hamburgers from the local fast-food shop nearby.

Uncle Soap spent most of his time hunched over the personal computer he had set on the round table in the middle of some paper stacks in what was a dining room. The chair he sat in creaked and squeaked constantly. He fidgeted all the time. I didn't really notice it until after my parents never came back. Then, everything was magnified. I wanted to go home, and see my mom and dad, and this desire made everything harder to cope with. By the end of the week, I had taken to hiding in the stacks of paper, and not coming out except to eat.

I think it might have gone on that way, but a short while after Uncle Soap and I started having troubles, Social Services stepped in.

# PART THREE

*Elton John — Saturday Night's All Right for Fighting*

M Y FAMILY HAD BEEN GONE ABOUT TWO WEEKS, and no one had seen them. Uncle Soap's calls to the police had raised flags, which brought Social Services in. They immediately declared Uncle Soap's place "unlivable".

Despite loud and angry protests from both me and Uncle Soap, I was taken away by a woman in a blue dress suit and a man in a brown suit. I can still see them. It was one of the most traumatic days of my life. I was hauled off, under the man's arm, and placed in the back of a white car. The doors locked immediately when the man closed the door.

The details are stark, and fuzzy, at the same time. The terror of being torn away from the only family I'd known was almost overwhelming. I could only think about escaping. When the man in the brown suit finished driving to the orphanage, I darted as quickly as I could towards the open door. I was caught easily by the man, who had been expecting this. I was corralled as easily as one might think a five-year-old would be when trapped in the back seat of an automobile.

The man grabbed me by the hair and around my waist. His grip on my hair kept me from biting him, which he'd probably had experience with before. He yanked on my hair as I struggled, keeping my neck and back arched as he carried me to a small room. It was a pale blue, and had a table, two chairs, an overhead light, no windows, and only one door.

He stepped into the open doorway, dropping me in the room, and remaining while I glared at him. He told me to sit in the far chair and wait until my "case worker" could talk to me. I remember him saying, "Bye, kid." Then he closed the door. I never saw him again.

The case worker startled me by knocking on the door. Her voice was quiet, and reminded me of a mouse. She asked if she could come in to talk to me, ignoring my loud "No!" by opening the door and stepping through. She closed the door behind her, locking it. I knew attempting escape would be fruitless; I couldn't get through the door.

She sat down in the other seat, tapping the desk with a thin green folder. She had on a business suit that looked like the other woman's blue one, only in pale pink. She had dark brown skin, and an accent that I didn't recognize. She said her name was Bethea, pronounced *Beh-thee-ah*. She talked about how hard it must have been living in that filthy, cluttered apartment. She said that Uncle Soap couldn't take care of me anymore because he wasn't related. I would be sent to a family, a foster home, until they could set me up with a real family who would be willing to adopt me.

I did not want to be adopted and go to a foster home. I wanted to go back to MY home. I wanted to see my mom and dad. I wanted to see Uncle Soap. I wanted to be away from all these strange people.

But my wishes weren't worth anything. The state placed me in a foster home, and it turned into a disaster. It was too soon after losing all the people in my family. I acted out, broke things, attacked the other children, and screamed constantly, until the foster parents threw up their hands and sent me back to the orphanage.

*See ya, don't let the door hit you in the ass when you leave.*

From there, it was one bad stop after another. Some of it was my fault. I couldn't get past that my parents had left me. I was convinced that they were alive somewhere, enjoying life after ditching me at Uncle Soap's. It was my fault that they left; my fault they never came back. Then it was their fault, and I took my anger out on anyone around me. I told stories, lies, about my parents. That they were secret agents, and had to leave me behind. Or, that they were wealthy beyond imagining, and had to leave me behind to keep me safe from kidnappers.

Each story was more outlandish, more improbable. I told them, because the truth I saw was that they didn't want me. I wanted an excuse that I could have why they didn't want me. The lies were for others, but they were mostly for myself. It hurt, and the hurt settled into a routine of more and more anger and behavior problems leading up to the night that destroyed any chance of me ever being adopted.

I was twelve, and a six-year veteran of the Social Services process. My latest foster family were known as strict, but fair, disciplinarians — supposedly perfect for problem children in the system. I was sent out to them to curb my violent tendencies. The stay lasted one day.

The father, Charley, was a shooting safety instructor, and a former Navy veteran. He was a head taller, and twice as massive, as I was, with black hair sprinkled with grey. His wife and partner, Kris, was my height, and stocky. She had blonde hair, and liked to dress up in fatigues. That was my first infraction: I laughed at her.

Charley immediately grabbed me, slamming me against the wall. He shouted the question, "Did I think it was funny?".

Being rebellious, and not realizing exactly what I had been placed in, I said "Yes."

Charley backhanded me across the face, knocking me into the kitchen.

The kitchen walls were papered in a pale yellow with light, violet-colored flowers. White counter tops ran all the way around from the archway into the kitchen from the living room, making a single gap at the door to the garage, then continuing back around to the archway. A second slap rocked my head to the right, and I saw the butcher's block with all the protruding handles.

I grabbed the chef's knife, and attacked. I think that Charley, for all his self-defense training, expected me to charge in. I did, but pulled up short, and slashed his arm wide open. He screamed, which brought Kris running. She charged into the kitchen, saw Charley's slashed arm, and me with the knife. I remember seeing her eyes harden. Then she reached behind her back like she was going to pull a pistol or knife.

I didn't wait. Two quick steps had me past Charley, and I stabbed Kris low in the stomach. She folded over the knife, and Charley hit me hard from behind.

Say goodbye to the orphanage, and hello to Juvenile Hall.

Kris and Charley hired a lawyer to get me tried as an adult. I later found out I'd killed the baby in her; it was only weeks old. The knife severed the small sac it was growing in. I was sentenced as a juvenile, due to my age, and probably because of the beating Charley gave me after I passed out.

I was sent away to the Palmerton Juvenile Detention Complex.

# PART FOUR

*Everlast — What it is*

I NEVER GOT TO SAY GOODBYE to anyone at the orphanage and, honestly, I didn't much care. The place wasn't home. Palmerton was a lot like home, only bigger — and lots more crowded.

The building was a re-purposed elementary school. There was a map at the entrance, with a "You Are Here" arrow right at midpoint between two large squares. The main entrance was between the two main buildings connected by a long hall that fronted the gymnasium-cafeteria. This made the place look kind of like a dumbbell from overhead. The dorms for the boys were in the west dumbbell; the girls in the east. Never did we see the other side. The powers that be declared us to be unfit for each other's company.

The dorm rooms were crudely bricked in place without altering the original classroom dimensions. A small straight hall ran from the door to the interior rooms, made up in four long rectangles per each former classroom. Two 'guests' shared each room. At capacity, we were told the Palmerton could hold one hundred and twenty of each sex.

Outside was a "rec field". It was two football fields wide, and one long. Sickly green grass grew in patches here and there, seemingly at random. There were no trees. The back wall was fifteen feet of smooth cement with coiled razor wire at the top. Cameras were mounted on each of the corner towers, which also controlled eight drones that hovered and darted overhead.

I still had vague memories of mom and dad, yelling, and a place with a lot of dry dirt around what we lived in. Palmerton was a lot like that, and I fit in there more than anywhere else since I had been taken away from Uncle Soap.

Everyone was out for themselves, and that suited me just fine. It was fight, or get bullied; predator, or prey. I wasn't an alpha, but I was close. No one fought with me if they didn't have to, and the perks for protecting others from some of the lower-level predators kept me in things like flasks of alcohol, cigarettes, iPods ... you get the picture.

I was the guest of Palmerton until I turned eighteen, and then my juvenile records were sealed, and I was kicked out onto the streets, with an obligatory stay in a "halfway house" to help me re-integrate with the world.

Truth be told, I was reluctant to leave Palmerton. I'd had a sweet setup there, and saying goodbye was like being taken away from Uncle Soap all over again.

The halfway house was a surprise — I mean a real surprise. The halfway house, called The Draper Center, was a series of four triplex homes nested at the end of a *cul-de-sac*. Whoever sent me there also sent my juvenile records. I don't know if that's standard or not. All I know is the boss, one Kesha Harkasse — whom everyone referred to as "Hardcase", took me aside, in an eerie replay of my confrontation with Charley.

She slammed me against the wood-paneled walls, compressing my chest with a finger the size of a bratwurst sausage, and snarled whether I was going start trouble by trying to stab her staff?

Her glare, and the taser in her other hand, convinced me not to smart-mouth.

She got a quiet, "No."

Thereafter, every day we checked in for work around the house. Things like cleaning toilets, mowing the yard, cleaning up gardens, painting, basic carpentry, and actually learning plumbing, filled my day from morning to mid-afternoon. Then, we gathered for lunch, talked about our past. Needless to say, no one really opened up about much.

Hardcase kept a sharp eye on me, and on a lot of the other kids. I didn't like her much after our first little chat, but she did keep everyone on their toes: working, studying, and getting ready to head out of the Draper and into the big, wide, scary, real world.

It was a month after I started there, that Harold "Hal" Matchick "graduated". Hardcase called us all together in the main house of the Draper, and announced that Hal's mandatory stay was completed. He'd found a mechanic's job away from any former relationships, and away from any other ex-cons. He had full-time employment, and would be heading back to school on a scholarship of some kind. He'd really tried hard and it paid off, big-time.

Hardcase got a cake, and soda (no booze, because that's against policy), and snacks. It actually was a good time, and the good-bye party really was like he had gotten over the hump and on his way back to a real life away from Juvie — and especially away from the real prison system. For one shining moment, we saw a dream come true.

That night, with the glow of the dream still alive in me, I saw a chance to change. Hal had made it; that meant I could make it. I just had to buckle down a little and get with the program. Some of the guys were already talking about doing the same thing I was thinking about: getting serious about the future. It's said that nothing breeds success like success, and we'd seen it first-hand, and wanted our own success story.

There's another old saw that says, "No good deed ever goes unpunished." That's what happened that night, but we didn't learn about it until weeks later. Hardcase thought the information would be too devastating so soon after seeing Hal pull it off. She kept it to herself, and the staff kept it in the dark too.

The story is Hal had gone home that night, to see his folks, and share the good news. He took a taxi to his folks, on the edge of Groveland. Groveland was a viciously poor part of town, made up of winding roads, old dying trees, and old base housing for the former wiring factory.

Hal got out of the taxi and was immediately spotted by old acquaintances in the 'hood. These belonged to a different gang than Hal did when he went into Juvie. Hal had 'tuned up' a couple of them before going in. Grudges die hard on the streets. This one was no exception. They got together and stole a car, then parked across the street from Hal's folks. As the taxi pulled up, Hal waved goodbye to his folks. That was the last thing he did.

The crew in the car opened up with pistols and a semi-auto-shotgun. The 'double-oh' buckshot knocked him down. Hal was hit by a number of rounds, both buckshot and nine-millimeter. He was dead before he finished falling. His parents were killed in the barrage, and his sister had her legs paralyzed by a stray nine-millimeter round that passed through the siding and lodged in her spine. It was one of those "What the heck?" things that you expect in a book, but not in real life.

# PART FIVE

*Uncle Kracker/Dobie Gray — Drift Away*

NOT KNOWING OF HAL'S MURDER AT THE TIME, I'd taken his example to heart. I pushed a little harder, worked on my GED classes, just like Hardcase wanted. I started going out more, looking at jobs. I talked to people rather than fought with them. It was different, weird. My whole world changed from one made with insults and fists.

I wasn't always looking over my shoulder for enemies. Now it was people genuinely pleased to see me — Hardcase most of all. With my metamorphosis, she changed too. One change fed the other, I guess.

The fact is that we — and I mean most of us in the Draper — actually looked forward to getting a new chance. Hal's example gave that to us. Hardcase was smart enough to keep the ball rolling and, instead of one, she had seven of us ex-juvenile delinquents that had seemingly changed our ways. I say "seemingly" because, after I "graduated" from the Draper, I lost track of everyone.

That's deliberate, by the way. No ties means no temptation; no one pulling you back into the life you had before. A clean break in every way. For me, it worked. I got my GED while at the Draper, and the party was for three of us. There was a lot of swapping stories and back-slapping kind of stuff. This was a goodbye to remember. Hardcase had to still get on us about our work, and she promised "holy hell" in spades if we backslid. I miss her.

I think her "tough-but-fair" attitude replaced my idea of what a mom was. Even now, I look at her as the mom I hadn't had before. It's a warm, nostalgic feeling, filled with little things like coffee in the morning, cleaning dishes — stuff you overlook in the normal course of a day. They mean more now, a good warm memory that overrides the harsh comparison with my own folks.

Because my records were sealed at eighteen, I had no criminal record as an adult. I gravitated to firefighting, convinced that was the best fit for me. Six months and four days later, I graduated third in my class. I got assigned to Firehouse Fifty-Eight, ironically, out near my folks' old trailer park. I didn't think much of it at first. Fire calls kept me busy, and the daily routine of cleaning the trucks, checking equipment, and going to the gym to push my strength, occupied my days fully.

It was the week-on, week-off routine that started me on my personal quest to find out what happened that night. At loose ends again while off-duty had me search for a way to fill the time. I got into camping. Big Bend isn't all that far away: just head east on Interstate Ten, then turn on State Ninety and, an hour later, you're at the entrance. There are always plenty of places to camp and hike. I got a metal detector too.

I'd read about all those people finding old coins in the ground, and thought that would be a way to spend the time during camping. Find a spot to camp, then wander about with the metal detector and see what I'd find. I got lucky right off, finding an Eisenhower dollar under about a foot of sand in a dry wash. Then it became more of small discoveries, like a jar lid, a rusted can, tossed pull tabs, thrown beer cans, and some loose change. All of this, I think, was me attempting in some way to connect with my parents.

I'd lay in my sleeping bag out under the stars in the bed of my pickup and wonder at the sky. Did my folks look at it the same way I did? Were they still around? I didn't think they were, but hope springs eternal.

It was six months after I'd started my camping habit, that the bug got me. Someone, somewhere, had to know something. The most obvious choice would be those who hung around my folks, and the most obvious one was Uncle Soap.

Ten years is a long time to lose contact, but Uncle Soap was surprisingly easy to find. He still lived in the same apartment, with all the same cluttered stacks of papers and barely wide-enough trails between them to the front door and the other places in the cramped one-bedroom. That I remembered his real name was a surprise. I never remembered hearing it. But Sonomorous Apijillo was unique enough to stay buried in my memories until the search began.

Despite his name, Uncle Soap didn't know a word of Spanish. I've never heard him utter one word of it. During my search for him, I found out a few things that made sense, given what I remembered of Uncle Soap. He was a researcher, primarily focused on political trends. He never worked anywhere except on the internet. He used a number of privacy sites to keep his ID hidden away from detractors and disgruntled employers.

In short, Uncle Soap loved to throw his opinion (usually well thought out and documented) at his employers — whether they wanted the truth or not. He was one researcher that didn't slant his work, and this "quirk" had gotten him a lot of research gigs for large companies — and a lot of irritation from the same companies because of his refusal to write "favorable" reports about their activities and attempts at influencing the public. He was, in his own quirky way, a bit like Diogenes: shining a lamp and looking in the corners of the 'net for the truth.

The day I went to see Uncle Soap started warm, and heated up from there. It was past the one-hundred mark on the thermometer when I pulled into the old apartment complex. The stucco walls were cracked. Here and there some paint had been slap-dashed on over caulking, but the difference between the fresh coat and the old faded one made the place look like a patchwork of shades of brown. The sidewalk slanted to the right as I started into the complex from the dirt parking lot. Dust kicked up with my steps until I reached the angled concrete.

It was so familiar that I shivered, regressing to the lonely, angry nine-year-old that I'd been. The screams of rage, and the feel of the social worker's hold on me was real around my waist. My breath shortened as my heart sped up. It took some deep breaths to slow my mind down and to banish the ghosts that choked my breath.

It was with a lot of mixed feelings that I walked to Number Fourteen and knocked. Uncle Soap opened the door to the extent of the safety chain, and then peered out at me. His face was much like I remembered: rounded, with grey three-day-old stubble, a balding head, and a rotund body that was more gaunt than my memories of him. He blinked bloodshot eyes, and grumbled if I had the right address.

When I didn't answer right away, he glared at me, and asked if I was a dumbass mute. In truth, I couldn't answer. I'd started choking up the moment the door had opened. The tears running down the edge of my nose caught his attention. His irritation gave way to puzzlement, then a dawning realization. His eyes widened. The door slammed shut in my face, the chain was noisily unlatched, then the door all but flew open as Uncle Soap stared hard at my face, his own eyes going misty with recollection.

Tears began leaking along his nose as he reached for me, fingers brushing my cheek. He was so small. In the intervening years, I'd grown, and now overtopped him by a full head and shoulders — a far cry from looking up at the big, round man of my youth. The fierce hug broke the dam, and I folded over his shoulder, crying my heart out as his own tears soaked the front of my t-shirt. I was a child again, and my Uncle Soap was here. Everything was all right.

I don't know how long we embraced, rocking and crying together. It felt like forever, and an eyeblink. Immediate, and timeless. The ghosts of the past wrapped around me like Jacob Marley's chains in *A Christmas Carol*. I couldn't stop now, even if I wanted. The chains of the past weighed too heavily on me to do anything else.

Uncle Soap gave one last, loud sniffle, then pulled me through the faded yellow door, into the world of paper stacks and pathways. Nostalgia rose up like a long-lost friend, and enveloped me in a dry, musty scent, laden with memories.

Still being led by the hand, I followed Uncle Soap through the maze of waist-high stacks of paper to the surprisingly clean and tidy kitchen. It was one of those incongruous things that you might not notice for ages, but Uncle Soap's place, despite the clutter, was actually very neat and clean.

There was no accumulated dust on his stacks of papers, or on the tall Venetian blinds in front of the sliding glass door. Somehow, despite all his clutter, Uncle Soap kept everything free of dust. Seeing this brought a surge of anger towards those long-ago Social Services workers. They took me away from the only family I had. My hands started hurting. I glanced down, seeing blood leaking around my fingers. I'd clenched my hands so hard my fingernails cut my palms.

Uncle Soap noticed too, and his face scrunched up with worry. He asked if I was all right.

That was a real hard question right then. I was tense with suppressed rage at the long-ago hurts, at the social workers, and most at my parents for leaving me behind. It took me a full minute to unclench my hands, and answer Uncle Soap.

He didn't really relax though. His face pulled taut with memories. I could see them flicker with each twitch of his cheek, every shift of his lips. He, like I, was in the grip of those long-ago days that this unexpected reunion had dredged up.

He gripped me tight in a sudden hug, bawling his heart out against my chest. I could feel his anguish in every shuddering catch of his breath. Somewhere in the middle of that, I was crying again, my own harsh sobs mixing with Uncle Soap's, making us sound like wounded animals shrieking for comfort.

I don't know how long we howled our pain into the empty air of the apartment. It was certainly long enough to turn my voice into a ragged, rasping croak. Uncle Soap was no better off. His voice was a sandpapered whisper when he finally tried speaking again.

We sat, heads together, arms about each other like life preservers in storm-tossed seas. We stood silently for a long time, slowly coming to peace with the emotional release that had overwhelmed us. The comfort of another soul that cared was so intense, so encompassing … it was spiritual. I don't know any other word for it — a spiritual connection, a spiritual healing.

Uncle Soap finally asked me why I came to him. I didn't answer for a long time. It wasn't that I didn't want to; it was because I couldn't. I didn't really know if I wanted to hunt down what happened to my Mom and Dad, for fear of what I might find — or, what I might not.

How would I feel if this was all a dead end? How would I feel if it wasn't? Is knowing better, or worse, than not knowing?

I was so wrapped in memories that I wasn't thinking, being totally immersed in those long-ago emotions of anger, desperation, and loss.

I finally, finally, managed to raise my head to look at Uncle Soap. His red-rimmed eyes were still moist with the remains of shed tears. He asked me again, with a catch in his raw, quiet voice, why I came to see him. It was a decision I'd wrestled enough. For better or worse, I had to know. Now it was my own damaged voice that whispered brokenly about my desire to know. I had to know. That was the only goal in front of me.

We talked: he wanted to test me, to make me certain this path was the one I wanted. I endeavored to convince him it was the only way to let the past go. We both knew it was already determined, but we both needed to make our case, to talk about our reasons — even though we knew they were the same. I guess people just need to talk mindlessly sometimes so that their real thoughts can have a moment to focus.

# PART SIX

*Eric Clapton — Tears in Heaven*

THE SUN WAS SETTING by the time we finished our discussion. Uncle Soap would help where he could, but it was going to be up to me to do the actual hunt. My job would give me access to past reports of incidents in the park, if one had been submitted. His delving into history and open records could uncover reasons, or some kind of activity, that created their disappearance. Knowing that might narrow a search. I thought it a next-to-nothing chance, but the operative word that swayed me was "next". There was a chance.

So we began, and I began to understand why Uncle Soap was so adamant about knowing my reasons. It became an obsession for me almost overnight. My parents. That long-ago creation of the empty hole in me threatened to burst open like an infected bite, and spew it's pain and anger through me once more.

I know I changed. The burning in my mind was something I could not ignore. One of the most powerful things is to have a solid goal, a quest for a holy grail. That was what it became. Every moment was focused towards my desire.

Uncle Soap found a few "trends", as he called them, that made him think that the park was being used for drug drops back in the day. That pulled memories of the scary man, the sudden money, and my parents big mood swings around "camping time". It made sense to me, but Uncle Soap argued that one thing did not make the another true. He needed more information before he'd say anything. I wanted an answer NOW. We fought over every detail he'd dredged up. I was convinced that the drug track was the right track. He wouldn't commit, because it was not definitive, not solid.

It was stupid. I knew it was stupid. My mind wouldn't let go of what I remembered. I refused to believe anything else. More than anything, I wanted my answer. Nothing else was important.

As you might figure, my performance at work suffered, and I relived all the frightening, ugly times that I experienced as a child. I'd turned back into that frightened kid who had been taken away after his parents vanished. All those feelings of loss, betrayal, and hate were with me all the time. My camping trips became crusades to slay the dragons that were consuming me.

I still found things with the metal detector — more coins, cans, and random bits of things. Everything I found hit me with the question: "Was it theirs?" Did my folks lose this camping? Did they camp in this spot, or over at another? What happened out camping?

I found myself seeking out the more remote, wild spots in Big Bend. I was hunting, but still unsure what, in my mind. It might have been to find something that I could definitely call theirs, something to put my faith in that I'd found them after all this time. Up to that point, all I'd found was junk with the metal detector.

Uncle Soap had been doing his "magic" on the internet. He followed up reports turned in by campers in a number of spots in Big Bend, checking for clusters of reports. We knew the weekend they disappeared, and that they were going camping. Incident reports of loud noises or gunshots were sparse due to the lack of wireless communications back then.

There were a few reports that Uncle Soap found in digging through old databases that had been made public. Based on the time they disappeared, he thought there were two places to search. I didn't have any friends, and Uncle Soap wouldn't leave his apartment, so the search fell to me.

A cloudless morning greeted me when I awoke. The still air held the promise of blistering heat as I exited my apartment. The dusty pavement surrounded me in a cloud of brown as I stepped to my pickup and got in. The engine caught immediately, and I backed out of the lot, then turned west towards Big Bend. The knobby tires hummed on the road as the miles disappeared under the wheels and, by mid-afternoon, I was at the Big Bend entrance.

The sun beat down, heat shimmering in front of the truck as I drove towards the first of the two locations. It was a spot I was familiar with. I was focused, ready to tear answers from the ground.

The campsite lay along the slope leading towards the South Rim, nestled at the southeast of the Rim, down near a dry wash. The area had been cleared recently. No scrub grew in or around the campsite. Salt Cedar and a few Willow trees clustered near the dry wash, as if waiting for the next rain. I was out of the cab of my pickup almost before the truck finished moving. The metal detector hung ponderously in my left hand, the headphones in my right. I clapped the phones over my ears and flipped the detector on.

The feedback squeal in my ears felt like spikes into my brain. I gritted my teeth until the detector finished warming up, then hit the discriminator button to select "Relics", and began sweeping. The coil moved back and forth, reminding me of a hound casting for scent. Small beeps teased my ears as I methodically hunted for my past.

After a half hour, I had to stop. I'd been gritting my teeth so hard that my jaw ached. The temperature had gone from a promise, to oppressively hot. Dust hung in the air with no wind to disperse it. It clogged my nose and throat, adding to my misery of the heat. I went back to the truck and pulled a gallon jug of water from behind the passenger seat. Half went to soak my clothes and get rid of the dust; the rest was for me, to keep me hydrated.

Too much water? Not in Big Bend. You do *not* want to get caught with too little water out here. That's how you *die*. All the tension of being so close to my desire had me tramping up through the site and back to isolated corners of it where a car could be buried.

You heard right. Buried. Somewhere I'd become convinced that my parent's car was hidden out here, just under the surface, waiting for me to come along and find it. That's what happens, when you sink your whole self into something without checking your common sense — dreams blow into irrational nightmares that swallow you whole.

I searched all day, over and around the campground. To be thorough, I ran a grid pattern: first north and south fifty paces, with a two-step separation. This made sure I overlapped with the metal detector my previous trace. It wasn't difficult within the campsite area to keep to the north-south lines, but outside the maintained ground, I had more trouble. Brush slowed me and, at times, was impenetrable to walk through. Irregular terrain made things tough, and some places weren't possible to reach.

Sundown splashed orange in the western sky as I reluctantly called a halt to my search. I had a sleeping kit with a large canvas tarp and two posts setting in my pickup bed. The posts went in welded circles at the front of the bed and into a hole at the top of the tailgate just off its center. This made a low tent out of the canvas by simply tying the edges of the tarp to the walls of the pickup. A blow-up sleeping pad in the bed with two wool blankets finished my "tent". I slept in the pickup, rather than on the ground. I don't like snakes, and Big Bend is full of them.

The wind remained still, or nearly so, which was pretty unusual. A typical day in Big Bend had wind, all the time. You were never without it — always trying to push, always shifting. Mild on the open ground, it got fierce in the deep gullies. Not having its constant presence woke me up just after midnight, convinced there was something just outside the tent. No crickets chirped, no coyotes howled — no noise at all. It was like the whole world was holding its breath, waiting.

A vague feeling of dread enveloped me. I sat up in the pickup and poked my head over the top of the tailgate in time to see a car rolling into the campground. It angled left and slewed drunkenly to a stop near my campsite.

The car was a Ford Taurus — an old beat-up nineteen-nineties model, like my parents used to drive. "What it is" by Everlast blared from its open passenger window. The Taurus bobbed and rocked on its tires as the figures inside moved about inside. I tried to stand up to untie the tarp so I could get out, but I was frozen in place. I was not a participant at all, but a silent observer.

The passenger door flung open, then back as it hit the stops and rebounded. A man kicked his foot out to hold the door from closing, like I'd seen so often. Dad.

He looked smaller, and more emaciated, than I remembered. He was wearing his old sleeveless black t-shirt with an orange Jimi Hendrix outline on the front. His faded blue jeans looked so pale to be almost white in the night. Mom slipped gracefully out of the driver's side. She carefully swung the door open, then closed. My breath caught.

She was shorter than I remembered, and thinner. Because of her constant dancing onstage, her body was taut and athletic. She'd discarded the baggy clothes, and was wearing low-rider jeans and Dad's red and black T-shirt. I never really remembered seeing her without all the baggy, shapeless clothing. It was like seeing a butterfly after it had crawled out of a chrysalis. She walked around the front of the car and hugged Dad. They held each other for a long moment before separating.

Dad walked towards the high side of the campground, then nodded, and walked back. He whispered something to Mom, who was pulling the tent out of the trunk. The two of them carried the tent to the area that Dad had looked at earlier, then dropped the tent and commenced setting it up. Once the mushroom-looking tent was assembled, Dad walked back over to the car, pulling a cylinder with three legs on it from the trunk.

He walked halfway back to the tent, yelling something to Mom, who pointed downhill towards the large dry wash. Dad shrugged, and smiled, then trotted down slope. He walked at least of a quarter mile, yet I could see him clearly, as he set the cylinder down on its legs, then pressed a button on the side. On the top of the cylinder, a red light lit up, and Dad trotted back to the tent, a big grin on his face. He entered the tent where Mom was, and the tent shuddered energetically as they made love to each other. The tent quieted down after a while, and dad trotted back out to the device and turned it off.

He left the device off all the next day as he and Mom stayed around the tent, gathering firewood, built a fire pit from rocks, began drinking, and then shooting up. Through it all I was the silent sentinel, never moving, but always bearing witness.

Dad sat on the biggest rock, his teeth gritted as the needle slid home between the big and middle toes. The plunger depressed as he tilted his head back, a beatific smile forming on his lips as the drug coursed through him. He capped the needle, dropped it in the fire pit, then walked back towards the tent. After he entered it, things sped up. The sun raced across the sky, dropping behind the hills as day shifted to dusk.

A glint in the north sky caught my attention. Then a flash of lightning lit the purple and orange clouds off in the distance to the west. The object in the north reflected the rays of the setting sun as it approached. Mom and Dad's tent spasmed crazily, and Dad came running out, pants half pulled up. He stumble-ran to the object in the dry wash and flipped it on. The red light pulsed faintly as he finished pulling his pants up and ran back towards the tent.

Mom was standing out front, pulling on her black Rolling Stones t-shirt with the huge red lips and tongue on the front, watching the small airplane weave closer now that the signal was active. As the high-wing airplane flew in just above treetop level, a large canvas tarp was pulled back on the passenger side. The plane rolled to its right, and a large square package fell from the plane. A chute attached to the package opened immediately, and the box fell in the dry wash, not fifty yards from the signal device.

Dad and Mom had watched the drop with glee, dancing excitedly in place while the plane flew over. Dad took off for the dry wash as soon as the chute opened, running like mad. Mom followed gingerly; she was barefoot and the ground was uneven, with prickly pear cactus, low spiny brush, and other uncomfortable things that would be painful to step on. She stopped halfway to the dry wash, then turned towards the car, limping over to it, and getting in.

The old Taurus rattled to life, then backed down into the dry wash where Dad was busy untangling the parachute from the box. He pulled a box cutter from his pocket and sawed away at the cords holding the chute and package together. Mom knocked over the cylinder, then hopped out of the car, walking over to turn off the signal device, open the trunk, and place the contraption back inside it. Neither of them paid much attention to their surroundings. The first hint of anything wrong was the trickle of water around their feet.

Dad yelled something at Mom, who splashed to his side. The water was halfway up their calves as they tried to lift the box into the trunk of the Taurus. The water actually helped them reach the bumper, but they didn't have the strength, or the leverage, as the water rose past their knees.

The car rocked as the water began to push it downstream. The motion caught Mom by surprise. The bumper hit her knee. She lost her grip on the package, and disappeared under the water. Dad yelled and dropped the box, which started floating downstream. He turned, reaching for the box with his right arm, while leaning over and searching the water with his left for Mom. The car pushed against him in the waist high current and, for a moment, he held his ground. He abandoned the box and put his desperate effort into finding Mom.

I saw her hand raise up out of the muddy brown torrent for a brief moment. Dad reached for her … and lost his fight with the water. The car lurched like a metal crocodile, driving him down in the water. His hand appeared by Mom's, then they both disappeared as the Taurus floated over them, tilted, and sank as water poured into the open windows. I saw it flip in the raging brown water, its bumper flashing silver like a leaping fish, then it disappeared.

The water continued to rise until it lapped at my still feet. The dry wash had become a raging river. Debris flashed downstream. To me, it looked like lost dreams and hopes carried away by the power of the world.

Through all of this I was held motionless, unable to move, or feel, until both Mom and Dad disappeared. I felt Mom's last thought of wanting to see me, and Dad's despair of losing both the drugs and Mom. They were small flashes of pain, and regret — of wishes that now would never come true.

For a moment, there was a last wish, a final spark, and then they were gone. A last touch, a fading grasp at life. I was stunned by it all. All the pain, all the fear, the disbelief, the sense of loss, and the reluctant acceptance.

They were gone. Fifteen years of not knowing, fifteen years of "what if?", all of it, gone in one night. I don't know how long I sat there, watching the muddy brown flood rise, roil, then fall away as the water disappeared into the thirsty ground like a fading memory. The dry wash was once again a pristine sand bed: no plants, animals, car, or people.

Coyotes howled in the distance. The noise was unnerving. The cacophony of their voices matching the turmoil inside me as I tried to make sense of the nightmare. Noise.

I opened my eyes. The sun was still below the horizon. The sky was a clear yellow blue to the east, a dark blue violet to the west. Overhead was the deep, pastel blue of the coming dawn. I was sitting in the middle of the dry wash, near a half-buried portion of a large branch, or small tree.

A few small birds darted by, starting their own day of finding food. The only noise was the wind blowing softly, and a last fading howl of a coyote. I pushed myself upright, and faced the direction I dreamed Mom and Dad floated away with the Taurus. The piece of ground I was standing on was the place in my dream where I saw the Taurus disappear under the raging water. I shivered as a chill ran up my spine.

Was this the place? Were they buried here under the sand?

The sense of conviction that this was true had to stem from the dream, but I couldn't shake the feeling that they were there, under the sand. There was one way to find out: my metal detector. If the Taurus was here, there should be a large signal from the detector.

I slowed as I got back to my camp. Silence enveloped me. The wind had died, and I heard none of the typical morning sounds. It seemed that the whole area was holding its breath. All of its attention was on me, and waiting for what I was to do. The sense of a strange, life-altering moment felt heavy upon me — a diverging path that would define my direction in life.

I saw things in two distinct possibilities. One, I would find the Taurus, know my dream was a true past seeing, and move forward in a life that always hunted answers and reasons why. Or, I could let go of it all. Say goodbye to their mystery, and call my vivid experience just a dream, and move forward in the life I'd begun for myself.

Follow them, and hunt more answers, or let go and follow an unknown path. My hand was on the metal detector. It would be a simple thing to confirm that the dream was a true seeing. All I would have to do was use the detector. I could use it, and let go, say goodbye, knowing they weren't lost … or so I told myself. It would be so simple; and it was so tempting. I could prove my dream. Prove to myself that my Mom and Dad were …

I looked at the metal detector in my hand once again. A sudden soft breeze floated past me. Warmer than the air around me, it enveloped me like an embrace of a lover — or a parent. My eyes blurred with tears and my heart clenched.

My hand, still gripping the metal detector tightly, trembled. I closed my eyes, blinking the tears away, and made my decision.

# THE JIMINY

*This story really surprised me. It was one line in a different story that triggered me to write it. The main character in that story had weird dreams every night because the dreams were his reality. So this one started normal, then took off on its own direction right after the character woke up. I had a lot of fun following the twists and turns. I never really knew where the story was going. I made no notes, charted no ideas or scenes. It, like every story excepting "… And a Creature Was Stirring", comes from itself. The story just started whispering in my ear, and the only job I had was to write it down as it was told to me.*

# 1

TRAVIS HOAD LAY IN BED. The sunlight crept slowly up until it caught his eyes. Travis groaned and squinched them tighter against the irritatingly cheerful light. He heard the wind flutter the curtains, and the sounds of birds calling.

*I must have opened the window last night? I don't remember doing it.*

Travis sat up, stretching his arms over his head. The sheets slid down his body like silk to puddle in his lap. He yawned loudly and stretched his arms out.

*This feels awesome. I must have had a great sleep. Maybe I should keep the window open more often …*

He stopped in mid-stretch.

*My sheets never felt like this before.*

Travis cracked his eyes open.

The bed stretched a good eight feet to the end, and at least six to either side. Wrinkled around him lay blood-red satin sheets overlain by a soft blanket of navy blue. A window stretched from wall to wall and floor to ceiling. The curtains were pulled shut, but fluttered at its center at the bottom, where a window or door behind it was apparently open.

*Is this a dream?*

Travis quickly looked at his left hand, then bit down hard on the first two fingers.

"YEEEOOW!"

Okay, it wasn't a dream.

"What the hail is this place?"

The room itself dwarfed the bed, looking to Travis the size of a football field from the foot of the bed. The walls were a good, it seemed to Travis, sixty feet away to either side. The wall opposite the glass window-wall was black — not just black because of the shadow, but black wood inlaid with an odd silver filigree that he could see in complete detail, despite being so far away. The silver wriggled and wiggled on the wall, back and forth, creating what to his eyes resembled two wrinkled microwaved potatoes pressed against each other in a sad attempt at a circle.

As he continued to look at the door, a bright light snapped on over its top with the words: ARE WE AWAKE?

He tilted his head, wondering who the sign was meant for.

ITS FOR YOU, JIMINY, the light spelled out.

"Me?" Travis pointed at himself. *No, this can't be real, I'm still dreaming.*

The sign scrawled out in an irritated scribble: YOU ALREADY BIT YOUR FINGERS ONCE. CARE TO TRY AGAIN?

Travis scooted to the edge of the bed, then stopped.

*Where do I find some clothes around here?*

He shivered uncomfortably, realizing he was naked as a jaybird in a huge and fancy empty room. Naked. In a huge bed with blood red satin sheets, and not a towel or bathrobe to be seen.

Another thought intruded: *Where the hell do I get a beer around here?*

For the last sixteen years, he'd always started out with three beers for breakfast. It got him through the morning — through the morning at his rotten job, at the rotten, stinking job of setting the housings around air conditioning compressors. That was all he did for twelve hours a day, six days a week, fifty-two weeks a year: putting shrouds around air-conditioning compressors. He'd been put on shrouds as he was the biggest guy on the floor. It fell to him to lift the compressor and stand it onto its rack, then bolt the shroud in place so the next man could wire and add the fan.

Travis loomed six-foot, five-inches tall with a receding hairline of jet-black hair, and a round face. Because he was so tall, it was natural that he'd have a large body (with an equally large stomach), which helped him weigh three hundred and eighty-eight pounds. It made moving the large pieces of equipment easier when he had the weight to brace and pick the whole unit up to turn it, rather than have help. It also helped to have that weight so he could drink more beer and not get so buzzed.

IT DIDNT HELP YOU, DID IT? the sign flashed quickly.

That comment reminded Travis of his floor manager. The floor manager, or 'FM', was always down his neck, telling him he ought to be moving faster, and the beer buzz was just enough to keep him from dropping the shroud on the miserable floor and riveting the FM into it. Lunchtime would roll around, and it'd be six beers in his truck out in the parking lot to keep the buzz going for the rest of the shift, until it was time to hit the bar and really unload. He really wasn't a drunk; he just drank to take the edge off his problems.

YOU WERE A DRUNK, the sign flashed.

"I was not!"

YES, YOU WERE.

"Where do I get some clothes?!" Travis yelled at the sign, since it was the only thing communicating with him.

JUST ASK FOR THEM.

"Huh?"

*Ask? Does it mean someone delivers clothes?*

The thought had him going neck-deep into the luxurious-feeling satin sheets once more.

"How do I do that?"

He was getting used to this dream. It was weird, but at least it wasn't a nightmare.

OH, THIS IS NOT A NIGHTMARE. the sign printed in light blue.

It seemed to Travis that the sign seemed to flash with a smug "I know something you don't" attitude. Travis decided he didn't like that. It was time to show this dream who was boss.

He sneered at the sign. "So what is this, Mr. Know-It-All?"

GET DRESSED AND FIND OUT. The sign scrolled cheekily

"How the hell am I supposed to do that? Ain't no clothes here!"

ASK FOR THEM. the sign scrolled testily.

"Ask for clothes, just like that. Well, fine. I want some clothes!"

Travis waited, and then waited some more.

YOU HAVE TO ASK FOR WHAT KIND ... UNLESS YOU WANT TO WEAR A THONG BIKINI? the sign scrolled with what seemed a wiggling smirk.

"A thong bikini?"

The words had just passed Travis' lips when a sudden swirling rush of air swirled around him. He blinked as the sheets swirled up, then settled back down, sliding past the twin white triangles of cloth that now rested on his chest. His nether regions had a sudden funny, rubbing feeling. He looked down at the unfamiliar sensation. His eyes went as wide as dinner plates when he saw what was now in place over his chest. Travis screamed and quickly thrashed out of the top and bottom, his face pale and sweating.

*Oh my gawd, what the hell just happened? That was like some stupid comedy trick, only it ain't funny! How did they ... it ... get that on me without noticing?*

Suspicious, Travis looked back over at the sign over the door.

*I swear, it ain't doing nothing, but I get the feeling that it'd be whistling and smiling like a damn cat that ate a canary.*

The longer he looked, the more the notion seemed to be fact.

"You set me up," he growled furiously.

WHO, ME? HOW COULD I SET YOU UP? IM JUST A SIGN. The sign somehow continued to act innocent and scrolled.

Travis believed that not for a second.

*It was a dream, dammit! It was his dream and he should be in charge.*

YOURE NOT IN CHARGE, the sign printed slowly, that smug know-it-all attitude oozing from it once more.

That really chapped Travis' ass.

*If it was a person, I'd smack it up one side and down the other and really show it who's boss. This is a dream! Any moment I'll wake up and this stupid room will be gone and I won't have to remember anything, especially that ...*

Travis squeezed his eyes shut hard and compressed his lips into a thin line. He would not mention what just happened a few moments ago, to anyone, especially his best friend Harvey.

*I'd never hear the end of it, and he'd tell everyone else, and no one would ever let it go.*

YOU MEAN YOUR EX-BEST FRIEND? scrolled the sign.

Travis wasn't certain, but the room seemed to suddenly grow a little colder. He pulled up the sheets then lay back down, a cold sweat breaking out.

AREN'T YOU GOING TO ASK? printed the sign slowly.

Travis didn't answer; he had shut his eyes attempting to will himself to wake up and end this strange dream. He'd just started to relax when the whole room shook like an earthquake. The bed was stuck to the floor somehow, and never slid or shifted, but the same couldn't be said for Travis. The sudden tilt to the right nearly spilled him off the side of the bed. A lurch forward threw him up and off it like a catapult. He landed on the floor and skidded face-first into the far wall with a loud thud.

"OW! Miserable, moth**8&%@& **!!"

He was cut off in pained mid-rant when the room shifted again, throwing him away from the wall, and rolling him back across the floor and halfway to the bed.

*What is going on?! Did that freaking sign have something to do with all this?!*

He looked over to the sign, the bottom edge lit up and bluish light moved up and down looking like two hills growing then receding. It reminded Travis of a shrug somehow.

I HAD NOTHING TO DO WITH IT, JIMINY.

"Jiminy?"

Was that some kind of insult or put-down? A slight breeze reminded him he was still butt-naked.

"How the heck do I get some clothes around here?!"

I TOLD YOU: ASK FOR THEM, the sign replied with a smug flourish of letters.

"Okay, genius. How do I ask for them?"

Travis thought the sign suddenly looked, well ... impatient.

YOU ASK BY SAYING WHAT YOU WANT.

The sign scrolled the letters very, very slowly, and large, covering the whole height of the sign from top to bottom. It felt like it was trying to yell louder and slower, which made Travis more frustrated.

REMEMBER THE THONG BIKINI.

That shut Travis up, and he shifted to sit cross legged in the middle of the bright blue-green marble floor.

"What I want, huh?" Travis stared at the sign, daring it to print something.

The sign obliged. EXACTLY scrolled across its face with what Travis felt was smug satisfaction.

He hated smug satisfaction in people; they were always so stuck on themselves.

"Okay, I want a set of silk pants and a Hugh Hefner smoking jacket."

His naked rear suddenly felt a sinfully smooth cloth against it as a comfortable, baby-soft coat settled around him out of thin air.

He looked at his now-covered arms. "Burgundy."

YES, A SATIN BURGUNDY SMOKING JACKET JUST LIKE HUGH HEFNER, the sign scrolled with a bored flourish of letters.

Travis glowered and took off the jacket. It was his dream, obviously. How else could you explain Hugh Hefner's smoking jacket?

ITS NOT A DREAM . . . the sign scrolled with a series of contemptuous dots at the end of the letters.

Travis started doing a slow burn. If it was his dream, he darn well could get what he wanted — and what he wanted was his regular pair of Dickies slacks, his blue button-down shirt, his black belt with the Budweiser logo on it, and his Red Wing steel-toed boots. What he really wanted ... was to wake up.

He'd heard you could wake yourself out of dream by forcing yourself awake. Well, supposedly you could by hurting yourself, but he'd already bit his fingers and didn't wake up, so what to try next?

HOW ABOUT JUMPING OUT THE WINDOW? the sign spelled out in green letters.

The way the letters appeared had Travis wondering what the sign was up to now.

"You jump out the window first, then I'll try it, ya darn idjit."

*Hah, now if it's a dream it'll go sailing though those curtains.*

I CAN'T. I'M JUST A SIGN. it spelled out in white once more.

"Oh, come on, it's my dream. You're supposed to do what I wantcha to." He pointed at the window, a stern look on his face. "Go on, jump."

The sign flickered an annoying set of colors, then scrolled amongst them, I ALREADY TOLD YOU, I CAN'T. FOR ONE, I'M A SIGN. AND, FOR TWO, THIS ISN'T A DREAM.

"The hell it isn't. I ain't at home. I ain't in my reg'lar clothes. And I ain't had a beer. Ain't no way this isn't a dream! I am gonna wake up, get a shower, and get dressed for work. I gotta shift to pull. I ain't wastin' no more time with a stupid dream!"

He crossed his arms stubbornly and dared the sign to do something.

It did, but not what he expected.

# 2

T HE SIGN WENT LIGHT GREY FOR A MOMENT, then started scrolling images. They started blurry, but, as Travis concentrated, became clearer. There was a light, but it seemed distant. There were three men in dark blue jumpsuits, with a white and red patch on the left bicep. Stitched on the patch was a green cross inside a gold circle with the letters 'Goldsboro' over the top of the cross and 'Rescue Squad' on the bottom.

Two of the men knelt in his kitchen next to him. Vomit pooled on the tan linoleum floor near his head, and a puddle of blood under it. Travis could see his wife, Kimmy, talking to a police officer and pointing at a chunk of the white Formica counter lying next to his head. Travis winced internally as he felt the impact when he'd slipped after throwing up.

*Wait. Slipped? What the hell?*

His mind ran away on him as he watched the Rescue Squad members wrap his head with gauze, then slide a flat, yellow board with holes for handles on the sides under him. Three officers moved next to the three medical techs, then bent over, slowly lifting all three hundred and eighty pounds of him up.

Then they all shuffled out of his kitchen, and into the cold December night. The red-striped white coroner's van, its lights flashing, sat parked next to the boxy white ambulance. Headlights illuminated the tan police cruisers just beyond it. He watched as one Med Tech unbuttoned his shirt and pulled it open. The Med Tech grabbed the stethoscope from around his neck, then pressed the disc to Travis' chest.

The Med Tech was a young kid with a thin face and lean body. His wisp of a beard made him look like one of those skateboarding punks that rode over at the park on the weekends. He raised his hand and shouted at the others, while making made a circling motion. The team jumped into action, pushing Travis' body into the back with his shirt still open. The ambulance spun its rear wheel in the dirt, then dug in and rolled away, its red lights flashing. Travis watched it go down Drumhill Street, turn west onto 119th Avenue, and then out of sight.

*That was me?*

Travis tried to deny it, to convince himself that it was *just* a dream, but something in him remembered the slip and the fall. He lunged forward drunkenly. The stumble turned into a full dive and his head hit so hard he saw flashes. He remembered standing up, and seeing Kimmy's face as her eyes opened wide and her hands covered her mouth just before it all went dark again. He dimly remembered falling a second time.

"That ... was me?" He didn't want to believe it.

SADLY, YES, THAT IS YOU. THAT'S YOUR LAST MEMORY.

The sign seemed brusque, impatient.

NOW, ARE YOU CONVINCED? IF NOT, YOU CAN STILL JUMP OUT THE WINDOW.

Travis shivered, and stayed on the floor, looking down at his rotund figure in red satin pants.

"What is this place?"

THIS IS, FOR YOU, YOUR NEW PLACE, JIMINY. the sign spelled impatiently. THIS WILL BE YOUR HOME FOR A LONG WHILE.

"What?" The words didn't make sense to Travis.

*I'm stuck here? In this big bedroom where a word would conjure clothes out of thin air like a dream, and a stupid sign that disses me every chance it gets.*

I HEARD THAT. the sign scrolled irritably. YOU'RE NOT STUCK IN THE ROOM. YOUR OFFICE IS RIGHT THROUGH THE DOORS BELOW ME. the sign spelled out helpfully, then added a downward pointing arrow to emphasize the doors with the same odd silver scrollwork as the walls.

"I have an office?"

YES, AN OFFICE. WHY DON'T YOU GO SEE WHERE YOU'RE GOING TO WORK FROM NOW ON?

The writing had that "I know something you don't" vibe again.

*If it's another thing like ... me in that ambulance, maybe I don't want to go look. It might be one of those creepy haunted house surprise things that scared the crap out of Kimmy when we were back in high school.*

Travis stayed put, still in the maroon satin pants and smoking jacket, on the blue-green marble floor.

IT'S NOT A JUMP OUT AND SCARE YOU THING. the sign printed slowly. It actually seemed to be trying to act sympathetic.

*Yeah right, be my buddy until you can push me into the scare. Nuh-uh. Not this old boy. I've seen that, well, done that a few times, and I know how it works.*

SURE YOU DO. I PROMISE, IT IS NOT A JUMP OUT AND SCARE THING. the sign displayed in soft lettering.

*Really? Promise, huh? Yeah, right.*

"I got to have clothes first. How about givin' me my work clothes?"

There was a swirl of air, and he felt just like always.

The pants fit like he remembered. The coarse threads scratched a little, and the shirt was a little loose since he'd lost some weight, but they were *his* clothes, and he took a moment in the small triumph of his dream control.

ITS NOT A DR— ... OH WHY BOTHER, YOU WONT BELIEVE ANYTHING UNTIL YOU FACE IT HEAD ON.

The sign was back to the irritable, exasperated printing as the sentences flashed in sharp lettering across its face.

Travis patted the clothes to make certain they were his, then did it again just to be certain. He'd had a few days when he'd been so hung over that it took a half-hour just to make sense of which way to put the clothes on and get to work.

*I wonder if this is the DT's and I'm hallucinating drunk. That could be why I ain't in control.*

The sign printed . . . . . . . . . . as if giving up trying to explain or convince Travis of the error of his ways.

Travis ignored the sign as he stood up, noting his feet were still bare.

"Can I have my old Red Wing boots?"

The breeze tickled his toes, and abruptly cut off as the shoes formed around his feet in an eyeblink.

"Huh, that was slick. I think I'm getting the hang of this."

He looked sharply at the sign, expecting a snide comment to go traipsing across the sign. But for some reason, it remained black.

*Hah! Got you under control too. I must be sobering up.*

He shivered as he remembered watching himself being pushed aboard the ambulance, then he straightened his back and glared at the dark door with the weird silver inlay, and then again at the sign.

*Sober or not, it's time to really wake up. I bet it's been telling me to go through there so I wouldn't go through there. Well guess what you old flatface, I'm going through them doors.*

The sign offered no comment at all as Travis pushed hard on the door, which flew open and stopped just before hitting the wall. The other door followed suit and Travis found himself looking at a room he'd never call an office in a bazillion years.

It looked more like something out of a bad black-and-white space movie. The room was an unrelieved dingy grey all over the floor, walls, and ceiling. The room swept in a smooth arc from the entrance to either side, then joined up again, by Travis' guess, a good fifty yards away. This place was huge.

The ceiling wasn't one really. It was more a curve of the walls. The whole room looked like the top half of a globe.

*Hemisphere. I remember that from high school. Half a sphere. This room is a hemisphere. What the heck kind of office has a hemisphere design and no windows? And what is that contraption in the center? It looks like a raised floor with a microphone and some levers.*

Stepping closer, Travis saw it was, indeed, just what it looked like. The center of the room was a raised circular floor, about ten feet around, with an old-style diamond shaped microphone on a pole, and seven levers arranged in a circle along the "front" half of the raised circle. Two things near the microphone looked like ski poles, with big cushiony handles at their tops. Light seemed to come from everywhere, and nowhere. The grey-on-grey-on-grey walls, floor, and raised stage all were easy to see, but there was nothing contrasting to really focus on.

*Well, that thing was right. It ain't no jump and scare, though it's really creepy looking.*

Letters in vibrant neon colors flashed from the base of the floor to two-thirds up the wall and ceiling.

IT IS NOT CREEPY. I SHOULD KNOW. I LIVE HERE. JUST LIKE YOU DO NOW.

The sudden attack of color had Travis falling back onto his bum and backpedaling like a crab on all fours away from the center of the room.

After a second, he pushed himself upright and turned around. A blank curving wall stared back at him.

"Where the hell is the door?!"

Two sections of the wall opened towards him back into the bedroom. It had been cleaned up, the bed remade and turned down waiting for him. The whole room shifted again, and faint words gargled like an explosion of sound. Travis jumped.

THAT IS THE BOSS. TIME FOR YOU TO MEET HER.

"Her?"

*First this weird place, and now a lady boss? What kind of weird drunk dream am I having?*

The dome lightened as the room shifted and the disembodied voice grunted, sneezed and sighed. The first clear image was of an alarm clock. The time appeared as "06:30" in tall orange letters; "am" in small letters were next to the bottom right of the zero. A slim hand appeared from the bottom of the view and slapped the alarm, then the light dimmed as it all went back to the dim grey.

"What the hell was that?!"

THAT WAS THE BOSS. SHE'S THE ONE WE WORK FOR. the wall spelled out helpfully.

"You have got to be kidding me."

I AM NOT KIDDING. THIS IS NOT A DREAM. THIS IS YOUR NEW LIFE, JIMINY. the sign printed in tight, blocky lettering. It felt like it had finally run out of patience.

Travis knew he'd run out of patience with this stupid dream. He wanted to wake up!

"Get me out of here! I got a real job waitin'! I got to be on time or I'm gonna get fired! Let me wake up!"

The images from before smashed through his mind like a runaway freight train. He saw them repeat endlessly: his falling, the emergency rescue squad, being put in the back of the ambulance. Then new images flashed into his mind: a back room with three bodies on metal gurneys, a man entering, wearing a white coat, a full mask, and latex gloves. The man moved the first body on its gurney over to a machine that looked like an industrial-sized upright vacuum. He slid the body in place, then locked the gurney wheels. He picked up a razor-knife from a small side-tray and pushed the man's legs open. A couple of deft slashes and the man then grabbed two hoses with what looked like meat injectors on the tips and pushed them into the open wounds.

He turned on the machine, which then rumbled to life. He flipped a switch, and blackish semi-coagulated stuff started plopping into the metal vacuum. The man's body seemed to shrink a little as the stuff was sucked out of him. A second flip of the switch started a metal column labeled "Formaldehyde".

Travis watched the liquid in the column drop as the body was refilled.

Once he got some overflow into the red-black gunk, the man flipped the switch again, unplugged the body, and pushed it to a corner of the room. He then trundled Travis's body to the machine. The embalmer picked up the scalpel and pushed Travis' legs open. He seemed to mumble something and laughed, then cut deep into both femoral arteries in the upper thigh. Travis felt a twinge of sympathetic pain in his legs as the man sneered down at his lifeless body and stabbed the de-sanguinators deep into the open wounds. He started feeling sick as he watched his nude body treated like so much dead meat. The man finally turned to face Travis, who stared back at the familiar sneer: Harry Deeney.

Travis had known Harry since primary school — and neither of them liked each other at all. Harry and Travis were the two biggest kids in primary when Harry started pushing Travis around and, in general, bullying him. Harry had the advantage in mass, so he invariably won the fights when Travis tried to fight back.

Going home didn't help. When he complained about it, he got "Man up" from his dad, who refused to do anything other than watch TV when he got home from the railyard. His mom slapped him, telling him to quit complaining, that she had it worse than some snot-nosed son of hers. He shut up and never talked to them about school stuff again.

Travis had a growth spurt in middle school, and Harry went from being the bully to the bullied. Travis wasted no opportunity. He'd gotten sick of being bullied, and it felt so good to put it to Harry. He'd pushed Harry the same way he'd been pushed. It felt so good, being on top that he'd started pushing others around too. It was fun and, big as he was, it was easy.

He had tried out for the football team, and was easily the biggest person to do so — big enough that he pushed the varsity players around like they were grade-schoolers. Made a defensive tackle, he created mayhem on the other teams. He was the big man in school. The guy everyone knew. He loved the adulation and all the perks it brought him.

Then, when he felt he had the world by the short hairs, he blew out his knee in the last game of the season. The college scouts that had come to see him play left without a word, and he was left, another casualty of fortune. He'd gotten to asking for pain pills after the surgery to repair his blown knee, and started washing them down with beer and, later, hard liquor when the pain got really bad.

He'd gone through the next year in a haze of alcohol and pain medication. He felt drained, and surrounded by a soft fuzz that dulled every sense. Kimmy found him then. She was tending bar at the Lazy Horse across from the truck stop out West. He was a frequent customer, and they'd started talking. Talk in the bar led to talk outside the bar, and to talk at home, and to other … "adult" things.

It was Kim that told him to quit the pills. She didn't mind if he drank, but the drugs were out if he wanted her to stick around. She was three-months pregnant when they married and, a month later, when she lost the baby, they both started drinking hard.

Travis hit the bottle so hard, it scared Kimmy. He passed out one night and she called the Goldsboro Rescue Squad. Her instincts were correct, and Travis barely pulled through alcohol poisoning. That seemed to give him a wake-up call. Travis was desperate to get back on his feet and take care of Kimmy. He got off the bottle and was sober until he started working for Hillaney Manufacturing, a company that built air conditioners. His first six months there were okay, then the new manager was hired: Mr. Robert Zillis.

Zillis was another of Travis' high school classmates. Like Harry, "Bobby-stick" was one of Travis' favorite targets in the halls. Travis had made Bobby's life hell for six months after "outing" him and Jeff Marisaak as gay. Travis took particular pleasure with pushing Bobby into his locker. He'd shattered

Jeff's jaw when Marisaak tried to "rescue" Robert from Travis' humiliations. Robert was pulled out of school by his parents after a suicide attempt, and that was the last Travis saw of him until Robert was hired as the manager at Hillaney.

Zillis remembered. He gave Travis every rotten job that his position would allow him to. Travis started drinking again. Kimmy got upset, but Travis never drank at home, and was very conscious of his actions. Zillis was still his boss. Robert had tried to get him fired twice, but after Robert's boss called him on a writeup, he settled for just making certain Travis got all the deadbeats and castoffs on his shift. No one worked, and those who did got written up and fired. Travis needed the job too much. He hated it to his soul, but needed the money for Kimmy.

*I wonder how Kimmy is?*

Harry stabbed the two tubes deep into the slashes, then spit on him as he turned on the machine. The blackish red sludge glopped into the tank as Harry turned to stare out the window. When the machine's light flashed, he flipped the switch and pumped the embalming fluid into him. He felt the faintest burning sensation on his skin as he watched this, and then the vision abruptly ended like a light being turned off.

The suddenness of the change disoriented him, and Travis dropped to one knee, waiting for his head to clear. This gave him a good look at his inner thigh: a long, deep wound ran across the inside. Fear spiked through him as he recalled the vision.

*I can't be dead. This is a dream! It's a dream! I'm going to wake up and Kimmy will be there in bed with me. We'll eat breakfast and I'll go to work later! I've got to wake up!*

YOU ARE AWAKE, TRAVIS. the wall spelled out in dark yellow-brown letters. YOU DIED. YOURE DEAD. EITHER GET

WITH THE PROGRAM OR SOMEONE ELSE WILL BE PICKED AS THE JIMINY.

The last part raised Travis hackles. "Oh yeah?! I ain't dead!"

OH YES, YOU ARE.

There wasn't a warning. The floor of the room disappeared, and he fell. Cold chains began to form on him, burning his skin and hooking deep into his body, and, onto something more precious. A complete grey fog surrounded him. The sensation was disorienting. No up, no down, no reference of any kind — just a grey emptiness that seemed linked to the chains that grew ever heavier and suffocating. It was like being caressed by clammy hands on every part of his body. He tried to scream, but the grey turned dark and swallowed him.

Just as suddenly, the sensation was gone. He was back in the grey room, curled in a fetal ball on the floor.

*What the hell was that?!*

He didn't want to think about it. Even as he asked the question, he knew with an absolute certainty what he'd just experienced — and was willing to do anything to avoid having that happen again. There was no way he'd ever go back there again. The reality crashed down on him like a breaking wave. He remained on his side, shivering, gasping for breath that didn't come, and crying tears that never formed.

The wall screen remained a deep grayish blue. It didn't feel smarmy or laced with attitude any more. It felt watchful, concerned.

"I ... I'm really dead, aren't I."

# 3

THE WALL FLICKERED THROUGH A FEW DARK COLORS of brown red and blue.

YES, YOU ARE. YOU DIDN'T SURVIVE THE TRIP TO THE HOSPITAL.

There was a pause, then letters scrolled in light grey against the deep violet screen.

YOU'RE IN BETWEEN. THIS IS THE CHANCE TO MAKE YOUR DESTINATION CLEAR.

*Dead. I'm dead. No more work. No more beer nights. No waking up with Kimm—*

"Kimmy!" He looked at the wall from the floor, his face an agonized mask of loss. "Kimmy's okay, right?"

SHE WILL BE. RIGHT NOW, SHE IS DEALING WITH YOUR DEATH, AND ALL THE PAPERWORK THAT YOU LEFT FOR HER. the wall printed in tall, light grey letters.

"Can I see her?"

*Please, just let me see her so I know she's okay. She stood by me when I needed it, and I just took it for granted. I am so sorry, Kimmy.*

YOU MAY NOT. YOU'RE DEAD. SHE'S ALIVE. SHE HAS A LIFE TO BUILD OVER. YOU HAVE A JOB TO GET TO, JIMINY. the wall replied in soft, fuzzy-looking blue letters.

Travis started to protest, but the feeling of the grey started to ripple along his skin — or whatever he now thought of as his skin. The clammy sensation had him bolting to his feet, choking back a terrified scream.

I THINK YOU'VE WASTED ENOUGH TIME, JIMINY. GET UP ON THE PLATFORM AND YOU CAN START WORKING YOUR JOB FOR THE NEW BOSS.

Travis had finally decided it was some guy on a computer controlling the screens, like that old movie with the man behind the curtain. In truth, he was kind of shocked that he was so calm after finding out he was dead and Kimmy was in pain from his dying.

*I still feel things, but it's like it doesn't feel real. Kimmy's there, not here. I'm dead, and it's like another day at the job. Am I losing it? It doesn't make sense. Why am I not crying more over Kimmy? She needs me and I'd be frantic to see her. But now all I feel is regret, and a little sadness. But it's fuzzy, like it ain't real. And now I gotta go see a new boss — a girl boss? I'd be pitching a screaming fit, I think, if I was still alive. It all seems so distant now.*

Travis gave a resigned shrug and looked at the raised center of the room.

"I go there, right. Fine."

He stepped onto the platform and put his hands around the ski-pole things and braced himself.

Nothing happened.

"Do I gotta turn it on?"

WAIT FOR IT. came the answer in a mischievous sky-blue lettering with a pink background.

*Okay, now that just sounded weird. Is this a practical joke or something?*

OR SOMETHING came the written reply slowly across the grey wall in tall green letters.

Travis clamped his hands tight on the ski pole things as the room shifted. It was like being launched down a rollercoaster. The sense of contact the moment he grasped the poles was dizzying. Some kind of annoying pressure rhythmically warbled along his skin. He gritted his teeth in irritation.

"The hell is that? Some kind of alarm?"

GOT IT IN ONE, JIMINY. ARE YOU CERTAIN YOU HAVEN'T DONE THIS BEFORE?

The light-hearted tone, after all the agony of finding out about his death, grated on Travis. It was kind of a minor thing, though, as if the reaction was part of someone else's life, or perhaps a memory of what he might have done — if he was still alive. Travis almost lost his grip on the poles as the lurching increased, then the grey faded out as a new panorama presented itself.

After the unrelenting grey, the bright light and colors came as a shock. A large, light blue box appeared on the wall screen. It took a moment for Travis to realize he was looking at a low dresser. The small white box on top of the dresser was an alarm clock. Its green numbers blinked off and on as the warbling sensation continued.

"Turn it off!"

The shout was like an instinctive push against the sensation. To Travis' surprise, a slim, brown arm reached out unsteadily and swatted clumsily at the alarm. He watched the fingers graze the alarm, half turning it, but not stopping the irritating sensation. There came another lurching shift to the room as the perspective changed. He looked down now at the dresser. At the bottom of the screen's display lay a thin pink cloth laying atop a pair of tanned legs. The view changed again as the screen narrowed focus to the alarm and slapped the top.

The rhythmic pulse quit, and Travis breathed a sigh of relief.

"So, now that happened, what's next?"

YOU, JIMINY, GET TO FIGURE THAT OUT ON YOUR OWN. ANYTHING ELSE WOULD BE COERCION. IT ALL HAS TO BE FREE CHOICE.

The letters appeared in black as they slid left to right across the view of a hand tossing a shapeless blue nightgown onto a bed with white sheets and a pink blanket. Just past the low dresser was another bed, also with white sheets and a pink blanket. The lump under the covers moved slowly, then the sheets were pushed up and back.

The girl underneath them wore a white knee length T-shirt with "I hate mornings" written in red block letters, and a cup of coffee underneath. The rainbow socks on her feet were neon splashes of colors against her pale pink skin. A black plastic-looking object with a blinking green light encircled her left ankle.

*What is that? Some kind of — oh yeah, I remember seeing that on a cop show. It's an ankle bracelet with a tracker in it.*

The realization that the girl had one made Travis curious about his — *her, it's a her, not me* — leg.

THE BOSS HAS ONE TOO. the screen scrolled in black block letters again.

*Great. So we're in prison. Or something like one.*

SOMETHING LIKE PRISON IS A GOOD GUESS. came the blocky letters again.

"So what are, uh, we … doing here?"

The sign waited for a moment before scrolling.

THE BEST THING, NOW THAT YOU'RE DONE FREAKING OUT, IS TO SHOW YOU.

The letters were rounded and green this time.

*Why does this feel like those shows when someone says, "Hey, it could be worse," then it is.*

The screen grayed out, then cleared. A glass door appeared in the center of the view. The view enlarged as the girl approached the door. A brick sped past her left shoulder as it was thrown at the door. Glass cracked and spider-webbed, but didn't fall, not until the brick was picked up and tossed again at the window. This time it shattered; the bits of glass falling to the pitted asphalt pavement. The room was dark as the view shifted inside. To the left, a cash register sat on top of a waist-high counter, a sign for lottery tickets taped on the counter's front. The dim light from outside revealed the yellow top of the counter and its red base.

The view suddenly began to shake as movement accelerated. It leaped and hopped the counter, grabbing a plastic dispenser that held scratch-and-win tickets. The container smashed on the ground, its plastic shrapnel scattering far and wide as a slim hand clad in a black windbreaker scooped the tickets up and out of sight. The view spun and blurred, then sharpened as two figures carrying a heavy chain wrapped it around an ATM machine. The view spun back as cartons of cigarettes were grabbed and thrown towards the smashed door. The ATM suddenly disappeared, dragged through the smashed door, taking part of the frame with it on the way out. It appeared to ricochet off the cement posts in front of the door and then was gone into the dark. Red lights flashed then turned left, followed by a shower of sparks. The view turned back again, and two more cartons of cigarettes were ripped from storage behind the counter, and then stuffed away into the windbreaker.

Then all action stopped.

Bright lights flashed and the figure was backlit. Its shadow had its hands on its head as a larger and stockier figure moved in the background. The shadow shrunk and sharpened as it moved, then the other's hands were pulled down, one at a time. The view trembled as this happened.

The view flashed forward to a courtroom made of green-gray linoleum floors, a raised section with a metal desk with a thick wooden top, and brownish folding chairs all over it. Six figures in orange jumpsuits stood in a row, each wearing chains. A pair of officers flanked them. The view shifted up. There followed moments of up and down motion, then the judge slapped the wooden mallet down. Fast forward again to "Dallas County Juvenile Detention" in silver letters mounted on red brick.

Fast forward once more to the room where the view had first started, back at the exact moment the pullover tee-shirt nightie dropped onto the bed.

"So? What do I gotta do?"

. . . . . . . . . . sped across the screen.

Travis felt like it was wiping a hand down a face, like he had no clue.

Well, dammit, he didn't have a clue.

AFTER ALL THIS, YOU STILL HAVEN'T GOT A CLUE, JIMINY?

"Hell, no. All I got is this weird ride through a screw-up's life, and all this peepin' on her doesn't set well with me. Do I gotta watch her pee and take a shower too?"

NO, YOU DON'T.

The view dimmed to the former flat grey wall. The wall stayed grey for a long time as Travis waited for an explanation. After what seemed like hours, the screen brightened. The scene in front of him wasn't the bedroom any more.

The sky was cloudless and blue. The open yard stretched away some distance before grey walls, with row upon row of barbed wire mounted on top, loomed up. To Travis, the walls looked twice a person's height without the barbed wire.

*This place ain't one that lets you leave — it's a prison.*

He looked around slowly. The screen turned with him, showing all sorts of young women in shapeless orange or grey shirts and pants that reminded Travis of hospital scrubs. No one wore shoes or socks; just pull-on slippers.

*If this is a prison, why such a nice room and a t-shirt sleeper?*

His thoughts were interrupted as, from his perspective, a tall dark-skinned woman approached.

She was about a head taller, Travis estimated, and likely heavier than him. She was about as wide as she was tall, with hair braided flat in cornrows along her skull. Her orange jumpsuit barely seemed to fit as she got closer. Travis felt nervous at her hard-eyed approach. The sneer on her lips, and on the two smaller girls behind her, had Travis suddenly very concerned.

*I wouldn't want to take her on at all; she must weigh as much as a beer truck.* He shook his head. *Her. I'm in her. I'm just a rider.*

YOU'RE A JIMINY, JIMINY.

Suddenly, Travis, had had enough. All the confusion, anguish, and anger he'd been holding in since learning he'd died came roaring out. He turned around and screamed at the blank wall.

"Listen, you lousy excuse for a television. I ain't no Jiminy! I ain't no cracker, or whitebread, or anything! So quit calling me that! I don't even know what that means!"

Everything seemed to stop, and Travis clenched his hands and jutted his head forward aggressively.

"Come on, you got a bone to pick, asshat? Bring it! I'll shove your teeth so far down your throat, you'll have to sit on something to eat it!"

The silence was so complete that not even an echo from his tirade came back to him. It was like the sound was just swallowed up. Travis' anger passed slowly as the moment stretched to a minute, then two. He had a sense of being under a microscope, totally laid bare, inside and out. He rubbed his arms, feeling chilled.

OKAY, MAYBE THAT WASN'T A GOOD CHOICE. BUT SERIOUSLY, YOU'VE NEVER SEEN PINOCCHIO?

The words scrolled in pink and yellow across the rounded wall.

Travis thought he could feel a sense of amazement — and a little chagrin.

*How does the guy do that? I've read a few books and no one could make me feel words like this guy.*

THAT'S BECAUSE IT'S NOT WRITING, EXACTLY. YOU FEEL IT LIKE I WAS SPEAKING TO YOU.

Travis thought about it for a moment.

"Really. So why the explanation now and not about …" he waved his hand irritably at the raised platform in the middle of the room, "… all that."

AH, THAT. YOU SEE, ANY INPUT ON MY PART WILL INFLUENCE HOW YOU ACT AND REACT. THEREFORE, I CAN'T TELL YOU. YOU HAVE TO FIGURE IT OUT, AND DO THE JOB — WHICH BY THE WAY, YOU'RE NOT DOING AT THE MOMENT.

Travis jaw clenched so hard he thought he might crush a molar.

"I gotta fly blind in a place I don't understand with a job no one can tell me about using a machine that no one will show me how to operate."

THAT'S IT IN A NUTSHELL. The letters spelled out on the wall in vivid yellow.

"ARRRGH! This has to be Hell! No one tells me nothing! I'm sick of it!" He glared at the screen. "Cough up some answers or nothing's going to happen!"

The screen flashed in a multitude of colors that played over the wall: splashes of red dotted with neon blue, and white squares half covered by dingy yellow splotches. The sheer three-hundred-and-sixty degrees of riotous colors washing over each other in a psychedelic display gave Travis vertigo. He dropped to his hands and knees and struggled to stay there. The colors seemed to roll through him, churning him up like an old washing machine, until he couldn't tell up from down. His vision began to grow dark as the churning sped up for a moment, then vanished so suddenly he dropped prone onto the grey floor.

*What was that?!*

THAT WAS A FULL OPENING OF YOU. The letters spelled out in tall thin white against a mauve background, WHAT YOU WERE WAS LAID BARE. I HAVE TO SAY, I'M VERY SURPRISED YOU DON'T KNOW THE REFERENCE.

The pressure rolled over him in a more speculative manner, and not nearly as invasive. It receded, then a square of white appeared: a grainy '5' in a circle counted down to '4', and then to '3', at which point there was a blip of light.

The square went black, then faded in again as a little boy — looking like he was dressed in goofy shorts with suspenders, and a weird little yellow shirt with a huge collar and blue bow-

115

tie instead of a t-shirt — watched this little thing in a tuxedo and top hat, look up at him. The two appeared to talk, then Travis thought he heard some kind of tune was playing. The little cartoon critter in the tuxedo hopped like a grasshopper, and started strutting along, hand on hat.

*What's he saying, I wonder. Are they trying to whistle?*

He remembered the conversation earlier: "You have to ask for it."

"Hey, does that come with sound?"

POINT FOR YOU. YES, IT DOES.

Suddenly the singing was coming across, and he heard the little thing say, "Give a little whistle," and then, a moment later, "Not just a little squeak; pucker up and blow!" which the boy tried to do, then another line, "… and if your whistle's weak, yell!" to which the boy answered, "Jiminy Cricket!"

*Jiminy Cricket?! He's calling me a cricket?!*

Travis started a slow burn once more.

*I'm a bug to him?! A freaking squeaky bug?!*

Then he heard the last part of the refrain.

"… and always let your conscience be your guide."

Everything fell together: Jiminy, the view he was getting, the "boss" reference, the smarmy lettering …

*I'm a conscience?!*

YOU CAN LEARN WHEN YOU PUT YOUR MIND TO IT.

The letters scrolled with what seemed a relieved-yet-irritated manner.

"Okay, so what can I ask for … I mean, besides clothes and sound? You said I had to learn to choose. So I'm saying tell me what choices I get to make."

The wall faded to black, darkening the entire room, then brightened once more. Travis found himself looking at the large black girl staring down at the "boss".

"So you got the J?"

Travis felt more than heard the answer.

"No, I ain't getting you any J — or nothin'."

Her fear filled the room like a suffocating fog. Travis' heart rate jumped. The screen brightened, colors and contrasts in light becoming more distinct.

He saw it all. He saw her choking fear, and her rapidly failing determination. She wanted to stay out of the drug trade. She didn't want to be here at all. The girl looked big enough to hurt her, and the other two behind her — bookend twins, if Travis was right — looked like real hard cases. Their eyes were, to him, empty of any emotion. Their faces didn't twitch even a little when they smiled.

The big woman looked hard at the "boss," her smile thinning as her eyes hardened. The twins behind the big girl caught the change and leaned forward almost imperceptibly, like attack dogs straining at the leash.

"That was the wrong answer, meat. TC, Mar, make her understand 'no'."

The girls stepped forward past the big girl, and moved towards Travis' point of view.

*Oh man, we're gonna get our ass beat. Okay, can we run. No, I'm too f— Can she run? No, not here. There's no place to go; we gotta fight. How would I handle this? Fake a charge at one, then hit the other one. If they're mean as they look, a hard kick to the knee'd be best.*

As he watched, the two girls closed in.

"Come on, girl. Step at the one on the right, then kick the knee of the one on the left."

He'd hoped that she'd listen.

# 4

*I* DON'T KNOW HOW THIS WORKS, *but the first time it was like she heard me.*

The perspective changed as his view lunged at the right girl, who took a step to the side. The screen whirled as the view turned at the other girl. The view jumped as a foot lashed out from the low corner of the screen and caught the girl on the side of the knee, dropping her. The view started to turn again when the screen rocked sideways and the whole room lurched.

Travis hung on to the poles for dear life as both he and the screen toppled sideways. The view showed dry earth on the left side as a foot at the end of an orange leg roared into view then passed low. The room lurched again. The foot retreated, then came forward again, and again, and again.

A second foot joined the first, then a larger, third foot. The screen shuddered as each foot slammed forward. Travis stomach turned over in empathy with each vicious kick. Her helplessness and hopelessness felt like a fist squeezing him.

Color drained out of the room. Everything faded to a grey, like watching a greyscale screen. Women wearing blue jackets and holding spray cans surged into view. The spray enveloped her attackers, forcing them to back away and rub at their eyes. The screen faded as one of the blue-jacketed corrections officers kneeled close in to the screen.

THAT DIDN'T GO LIKE YOU THOUGHT, DID IT? Bright blue letters scrolled across the now grey screen.

"I was trying to get out of it. You heard her. She didn't want to have anything to do with smuggling marijuana for those bitches!"

TEMPER, TEMPER, JIMINY. I AM NOT FAULTING YOU. MY COMMENT WAS MERELY OBSERVATIONAL.

"Don't call me that. I ain't no bug thing. If you want me, just call me Travis."

He glared at the screen as his mind tried to figure out what to do. He realized that suddenly he felt that this girl was his charge, and he had to look out for her. Somehow, it had become personal. The recognition of that feeling left him unsettled.

*What about Kimmy? I owe her. She put up with all my crap and never complained.*

KIM IS A GOOD, LIVING WOMAN. YOU'RE A WHISPER IN SOMEONE'S EAR, TRAVIS. YOU HAVE A NEW JOB. the letters spelled out in light pink and purple.

*Yeah, a new job.*

Again he was struck by the lack of emotion he'd thought he should have. The sense of loss was there, as was regret — which pressed down on him like a weight whenever he thought of his life.

*I have a lot to make up for. Maybe this is my chance.*

He looked at the screen, hoping that there might be a verification of this chance. The screen remained a blank grey.

*So I have to figure this out. Like hell. I ain't no thinker. I never even liked kids. This may be too much.*

THROWING IN THE TOWEL, ALREADY, JIMINY?

The words scrolled in a bright red outlined in a dark, dark violet that seemed to Travis like hungry mouths eager to bite into him.

"I — I ain't quittin'." His teeth chattered at the cold sensation along his spine as he looked at the letters, bright and pulsing like blood. "I ain't gonna quit. You said I had to do this, so don't get antsy."

I NEVER SAID YOU HAD TO DO IT, JUST THAT YOU WERE CHOSEN. YOU CAN QUIT ... ANY TIME YOU WANT.

The letters were in a deep maroon-brown that reminded Travis of dried blood, which nearly unnerved him. The fear seemed to make the letters grow, until they rolled all the way up the curved wall to the center of the ceiling. It felt like seeing vultures waiting for something to die.

"I ain't gonna quit!"

Travis locked his legs and prayed he wouldn't fall over. Despite the challenge in his voice, he wanted to be anywhere else but there.

YOU'RE NOT?

The bright red letters printed up, one at a time, floor to ceiling.

The effect was intimidating. Travis wanted to run, but his own stubborn streak kept him on the platform.

"I'm not, you sonuvabitch. I ain't runnin', and I ain't quittin'."

The letters shrunk back to a more "normal" size. The red faded to a pale pink that shaded to a bright blue at the top.

POINT FOR YOU. NOW GET SOME REST. THE BOSS WON'T BE WAKING UP FOR AT LEAST A DAY.

Travis thought about that information, then stared at the screen. "I'm not going to sleep until she's safe."

YOU REALLY DON'T HAVE A CHOICE. WHEN THE BOSS SLEEPS, YOU WILL SLEEP. YOU'RE PART OF HER, SO GET USED TO IT.

The letters were in a calm green that made Travis sleepy just looking at them. He closed his eyes and bit the base of his thumb to stay awake.

"No! I ain't sleepin'!"

YES, YOU WILL. BUT THERE IS TIME BETWEEN WHEN THE BOSS GOES TO SLEEP, AND YOU DO, THAT YOU CAN TALK MORE DIRECTLY TO HER. YOU MIGHT THINK OF THAT FOR THE NEXT TIME SOMETHING LIKE THIS HAPPENS. HER ACTIONS ARE GOING TO COUNT AS YOURS IN THE FINAL BALANCE.

The letters were a lazy, fuzzy purple.

Travis felt his feet shuffle towards the wall, which split and opened a door just big enough for him to fit through. He managed to shuffle to the bed, and fell wearily upon it. He saw yellow lights on the sign above the door, but his eyes were too unfocused to make out what they said. As his eyes closed, his mind tingled with the faintest sensation of a connection, then it was gone as the letters faded and he descended into the darkness of sleep.

The last thing Travis expected to do was dream. For him, it was a hazy sensation that cleared, and a young girl with dark mocha skin crouched a short way in front of him, her arms wrapped around her legs as she tried to stifle her tears against her knees. Travis felt a flash of something. The pink nightie dragged on the ground behind the girl, but did nothing to conceal the curves of her womanhood. Her hair was black, short, cut to shoulder length, and with a slight wave. It seemed whimsical, with pink ends. At the same time, it felt transitional, like changes were going on beneath the surface. The whole scene felt like one of despair and a desperate privacy, as if the girl was trying to hide. It tugged at him, yet there was a sense of unreality, of being connected, yet disconnected at the same time.

*How am I here? I don't remember waking up.*

He waved his hand, then tried to bite it. Nothing happened this time.

*This is a dream.*

He wanted to wake up, but the soft shoulders shaking as the girl sobbed touched him. He'd seen Kimmy cry the same way, perched on the edge of their bed as he tried in a drunken stupor to comfort her, realizing it was him causing the pain. Anguish and regret filled him, making his knees nearly buckle in shame for the hurt he'd caused while he was alive.

This was a chance to fix things. He started towards the girl, but he stopped short. Instead, he stayed two steps away, unwilling to close the final distance.

*Do I try? Or is this something I'd just make worse if I tried.*

The indecision tore at him, he did nothing but stare at the girl, paralyzed by her misery. The scene faded as he watched, followed by a vaguely unpleasant sensation, like a weight had been dumped on his shoulders. It was the last thing he remembered before his dream faded to black.

Light streamed in through the window, bathing him in a cold, discomforting light. The room shuddered slightly, like a large truck rolling by the house. Pressure, like someone tapping him on the head made him growl. He opened his eyes to see large purple letters on the sign over the silver and black door.

WAKEY, WAKEY, UP AND SHAKY.

Somehow the words felt a touch disapproving this morning to Travis.

"What now?" He started to get out of bed, and found that, like before, he was naked. "I want my reg'lar work clothes again." Something made him add, "… please."

A light breeze ruffled the curtains and blew across him. His clothing appeared like coalescing smoke and then solidified. He pushed off the bed with a groan, and tapped each boot with the steel toe to make sure he had them on. Satisfied that he was ready, Travis lumbered to the door. The sign was blank as the doors opened to the grey room once more.

Travis moved to the round platform, and grasped the poles to brace himself. He waited as the screen remained grey, with the faintest of darker shadows flitting across it.

"Is there any noise? I don't hear nothin'."

ONE MOMENT. the screen printed in a helpful, light orange-yellow, WE ARE EXPERIENCING TECHNICAL DIFFICULTIES.

Travis felt a sense to the room this time. The grey seemed to weigh heavier than yesterday. There was a sense of emptiness to it — which seemed ridiculous to Travis. He scoffed at his "feeling", yet it wouldn't leave him. The emptiness seemed to percolate into his skin, and weigh upon him, like regret.

The screen slowly lightened as noises became more distinct, shifting from a soft background murmur to distinct voices, and the sharp, clattering sounds of metal on metal.

"Hey, hon, you feelin' better?"

The wall irised open to reveal a dark, wide face atop a heavyset body covered in hospital blues. The woman wore a set of black-framed oval glasses with neon-pink bows that added a splash of color to her dark brown features. Perched atop her short frizzy hair was a white nurse's cap held in place by bright green and red clips. Her name, "Washington", was barely visible at the bottom of the screen.

"Y'all been out of it for a while, girl. Two days. Now that you're awake, we can get that I-V out of yore arm and get some food and water into ya."

*Two days? They kicked the bejeezus outta her.*

He wondered if that was what he'd felt. He shook his head and tried to will the view to change and show him more. Concern had him wanting to see the wounds and, at the same time, he felt a flash of anger at the abuse that landed her in here for two days.

*Payback, I want payback. They ain't gonna get away with this. They don't get to do that to me!*

He felt hot anger flow forth, and gasped as it was immediately doused by the empty feeling.

Something flowed across the screen: a profusion of color like the psychedelic colors before, but these were muted — colored in grey, blue, deep reds, and black. It felt, angry, and helpless.

A bloom of light orange blossomed on the wall. It reminded Travis of a wince. Other hues appeared, adding their own shades of orange on the wall, adding to an overall sense of pain from the whole being of what he had become a part of. He *felt* the pain more as an insult to the whole of him, intimidating and vicious. It pressed down on him, attempting to control his angry reaction. It was a frustrating sensation, one that bordered on despair, no matter how he tried to ignore or rid himself of the feeling. It felt like a lead weight on his shoulders.

*There's got to be a way. If it was me, I'd catch them one at a time and pound the snot out of 'em.*

He growled, and felt the room grow warm. That had to be the answer. A second thought entered his mind.

*I don't know what this girl is like. She looked kind of thin in the dream. Maybe if she looked in a mirror, I could see what there is to work with.*

As if she had been waiting for the opportunity, the slim hand moved to the call button, and a nurse came in.

"Hey, hon, you mus' be hungry. I can bring food in iffen y'all'd like."

She came over to the bed as the girl said, "Can I have a mirror?"

The nurse looked at the screen, which Travis now believed she was looking directly into the girl's eyes.

"Oh, hon, you sure you wanna look? You might wanna wait another day before you do that."

The screen waved back and forth as the soft, raspy voice said, "I wanna see."

The nurse shook her head and walked out of the room.

Five minutes later, she returned, carrying a hand mirror.

"The swellin's gone down some, but you took a bad one from them girls," the nurse said as Travis watched the mirror move to the girl's hands.

The nurse was right. The girl's right eye was nearly swollen shut. An ugly purple bruise started on her cheek below her eye and spread around it. Four butterfly tapes were across an angry gash on her cheekbone below the eye. The other side of her face hadn't been touched. It was a plain face, Travis noticed, with a few scrapes on its nose that hadn't been covered with a bandage. The lower lip was split on the right side of her face, the same as her eye. It had two butterfly bandages just below it to hold the wound closed.

She held the mirror as the other hand lifted the edge of the blue hospital smock, to expose her stomach. Its dark flesh revealed purple bruises with bluish purple centers more pale than the surrounding bruises. That was where the kicks had landed. Most had been hard enough that they were still bleeding slightly, which accounted for the change in color at the center.

Travis thought he'd be more nervous to see the girl's body, but rage was all he really felt. Those three women had done a thorough job of hurting her. The warmth seemed to increase, not uncomfortably, but like pressure was building — like steam beginning to overpressure the valves, like in one of those old movies.

*God help me, all I want to do is hurt them! I want to hurt them so bad!*

The breeze that started up sounded like a heated whisper in the room. Travis was still angry, but the whispering bothered him.

*Was there someone else here?*

He got off the platform, and tried to follow the sound. Against one portion of the curving wall, it got loud enough to hear just barely.

Travis strained to hear, and his stomach suddenly felt cold. His anger still burned hot, but a niggling doubt entered his mind as he heard the words.

*"Go ahead, they deserve it. They hurt you, hurting them back isn't wrong, it's payback. What goes around comes around. It isn't your fault if they bring it on themselves, right? All you have to do is take things into your own hands. Control your own destiny and make them pay the same way they tried to make you their slave."*

*Damn straight,* thought Travis.

*"Or,"* the whisper added, almost as an afterthought. *"You could just give in, let go. They'd make all the decisions and you wouldn't have to worry about anything anymore. Just give everything up, and then nothing could touch you. You could hide behind all their decisions and never have to make one again. After all, with the kind of power they have, yours isn't near enough to*

*protect yourself. And your cousin Nar'vell, he never was much to you. Get him to pass you the stuff and you'll be riding high in here. Those girls would need to protect you, because you'd be the source for everything, and you could keep a secret. Nar'vell wouldn't tell, especially if he thinks you like him. Just give up and let everyone around you protect you for what you can do for them."*

The voice was soft, gentle, and magnetic. Travis had to fight the urge to press up against the wall to get closer to it. He pushed away from the wall in confusion and tried to clear his thoughts.

*What, who the heck is that? I thought I was supposed to be the ... well, the guy up here ... the conscience thing.*

YES, AND NO.

Light spelled out on the grey screen in reddish-black block letters.

"What do you mean?" Travis asked angrily.

It was just like when he got here. Nothing was explained. He had to stick his foot in the crap to find out it existed. Why couldn't he just be told how to do the job and not have to go through all this stupid finding out the hard way.

BECAUSE IT'S THE RULES. NO HELP, NO EXPLANATION UNLESS YOU ASK. THEN JUST THE STRAIGHT TRUTH. AFTER ALL, WHY SHOULD I GIVE ALL THE INFORMATION TO THE OPPOSITION FREE OF CHARGE?

The letters had a condescending air to them, like someone who felt infinitely superior to Travis, which really pissed him off. It was the same way that twiggy little Bobby Zillis kept talking to him on the job — like he was so stupid that he had to be told how to tie his shoes every day.

*Forget it, I'm not gonna let that little creep win.*

OH, I'M GOING TO WIN, AND YOU'RE GOING TO FAIL AGAIN, JUST LIKE YOU DID WITH KIMBERLY — AND EVERYONE ELSE IN YOUR SAD LITTLE EXCUSE FOR A REAL LIFE.

"Just shut up, you," Travis yelled at the screen. His fists clenched and he leaned forward, jaw clenched, ready to rumble. "Come out where I can see you! We'll settle this right here, right NOW!"

OH COME ON. the light spelled out slowly, mockingly.

SERIOUSLY, YOU'RE GOING TO PUNCH OUT A WALL. LET'S SEE YOU DO IT, SPORT. THIS OUGHT TO BE REALLY AMUSING. COME ON, FATSO. WHAT DO YOU HAVE?

# 5

THE TAUNTING MAUVE LETTERS HAD TRAVIS SEEING RED.
In his rage, he drew back his fist and slammed it into the wall. It hurt. A lot. Travis didn't care, all he cared about was pounding that miserable, mocking sign into paste. Four more hard shots against the unyielding wall had him in pain that he couldn't ignore. It was then a sound reached his ears. Someone was crying.

It was "the boss". Her voice was making small gulping growls, as if frustration was bubbling out of her, and her helplessness was driving her into a self-inflicted frenzy.

"Let go, girl. I said let go! Marnie! Help! She got the scissors!"

The urgency of the words penetrated the red haze. Travis looked at the screen. It blinked off and on as her eyes opened and closed.

She was screaming, helpless rage pouring out of a throat made hoarse by the self-hate he heard coming from her.

"What the …?! What's going on!?"

I'M GLAD YOU ASKED, JIMINY. THAT'S ALL YOU, OUT THERE. CONGRATULATIONS. YOU MAKE MY JOB SO EASY, I HAVE TO LAUGH.

The letters were a deep brown-red like congealed blood. They seemed to pulse larger, and more ominous with each agonized, self-loathing scream.

It took Travis a moment to connect the information together.

*I did this. I got mad and she got mad with me. No. I made her get mad. My temper became her temper.*

The weight between Travis' shoulders became heavier than ever.

*I'm so sorry.*

His rage evaporated like mist. From the screen, he could hear the helpless sobs of the girl. They bore into him with the realization that he'd allowed it to happen.

He looked at the screen, hating it.

*Slow down. What you're feeling is part of what she's feeling. I don't know why, but it's like we're seeing things the same way. Or, are we?*

Travis started thinking more. He didn't like thinking. Reacting was a lot easier, but it also had gotten him a lot of regrets.

*Why am I here? That asshat sign said I was in-between. What did he mean by that? It's like I'm getting half of everything that's said. The other half isn't being talked about. And he's trying to get her to give in to that junk he keeps spewing. Why? What is the big deal about all that? What am I missing? I can't think. I get mad and want to hit something.*

Travis stalked around the round grey room clenching and unclenching his hands as he tried to understand more about the so-called rules that the sign wouldn't talk to him about. He'd occasionally glance at the screen and the hands at the bottom would close and open every so often.

Also every so often, the hands or feet or body would fidget, as if wanting to move, but there'd be a lurch followed by a soft whimper that stopped further motions. The seeming helplessness of the situation displayed on the curved wall, and Travis' own restless frustration at the predicament reflected his own thoughts and feelings.

He slowed down, his eyes riveted to the screen.

*Is that it? Is what I'm feeling being projected?*

He looked at the screen again.

*It did say that I had to learn on the fly. I hope that means asking questions, too.*

"So what's the deal? Why is she agitated when I am?"

There was silence for a moment then letters enlarged onto the screen. MY, MY, MY. SUCH A DIRECT QUESTION.

Travis ground his teeth and worked to stay calm. "Yeah, and what's the answer?"

Letters put themselves together from blocks and splashed pink against a sudden yellow green.

MORE THE OPPOSITE. YOU'RE JUST THE JIMINY, TRAVIS. SHE'S THE BOSS.

That explained a lot to Travis.

*If she's mad, and I get mad, then she's making me mad by being mad, right? So, if I try to be happy when she's mad, will that make her less mad? And if that's right, then I have to figure out how to keep it together when she starts to lose it?*

He continued to gaze at the screen. The view remained on the window. It felt so wistful, yet terrified at the same time.

*She knows they'll be waiting for her out there. What can I do to change the situation? My first reaction would be to catch them alone and beat each one to a pulp, but that's not gonna work. Size counts, and this girl's a twig compared to those thugs. I gotta be smart about this.*

POINT FOR YOU. scrolled across the wall as Travis was concentrating.

"Yeah, right," he answered without really paying attention.

*There had to be a way.*

He was on a time limit. It might be, at most, another day that they'd keep her in the ward. After that, she'd be back in the general population, which meant those girls would be looking her up again. Travis scanned the screen for things that could be used as a weapon — or modified into one. A sense of unease stirred as he studied the view on the wall.

*Why is this bothering me? If we have a weapon, we can protect ourselves better, right?*

He thought about that sibilant voice he'd heard earlier. The venom and hate hidden in the words seemed to slap him in the face as he recalled them. The more he thought about them, the less palatable the idea of a weapon became. He was so deep in thought that he almost missed the slight tremor in the floor.

Travis looked up, and saw that she was standing. The perspective was much more 'downward' as the girl looked at the IV in her arm, then at the tray holding a paper cup filled with ice and a clear liquid. The hand appeared at the bottom of the view, and picked the cup up. There was a faint slurping sound, and the cup was set back on the tray as the view shifted left and up towards some closed cupboards. They slowly enlarged on the wall screen as she walked towards them.

*What's she doing?*

Her arms reached up to the leftmost cupboard, then slowly began to open it. The screen swung back towards the partly open door and back to the cupboard rapidly.

*She doesn't want to be heard. Why?*

The doors swung open silently and her hands darted in and lifted various items for a moment, then placed them carefully back on their shelves. Travis closed his eyes and concentrated.

*I'm supposed to be able to feel things because we're linked, so why can't I now?*

He didn't feel anything, so much as *heard*.

*"Come on, there's going to be something we can use here. Rooms have all sorts of things that can be weapons."*

The vicious, yet honeyed words made Travis stomach lurch.

*"It's the only way: you or them. You can call it self-defense. No one will question it. It was something that just happened. You won't get punished. Protecting yourself is perfectly fine. If we're smart enough, no one will suspect a thing. Catch them all alone. A couple of quick jabs. It's just protecting yourself."*

*Oh god. She's going to kill them if she finds a weapon.*

Panic had him babbling.

"Don't do it! Don't do it! You don't want to hurt anyone! You'll be a killer and never be free again!"

Travis watched the screen as hidden underneath a roll of gauze was a small paper package about the size of a single-serving sugar packet. The cover said: "Scalpel blade #12". The yellowed paper covering showed a blade with a slight hook at the tip, like the back of a gutting knife. The hand covered it, picking it up, then transferred it close to the screen as the gauze was reset in the cupboard. The girl returned to the bed.

*"Yes! Good girl! We can make them pay for beating you so badly. Self-defense. That's all it will be. You'll be free. They won't be able to hurt you again."*

Travis heard another voice talking over the first one. He didn't realize he'd started until the first one quit. The wall fuzzed a moment. The hand was still in the view, still holding the packet with the blade.

"Com'on, you don't need that. Think, girl. If you get caught, you won't be just in here for a little while longer, you'll be here a lot longer. And the longer you're in here, the more chances those girls will have to get you. Just put it back, and forget about it. There are other ways to handle what's happening. You can't let it control you. One bad step and it's going to swallow you whole."

Travis continued to ramble in a near panic as he watched the hand waver. Indecision kept the hand from moving as he tried to convince her to put it back. A clatter of metal on metal had the hand, still holding the small surgical blade, disappear from the wall screen.

*No. no no no no. She still has the knife. She's going to get caught and that, on top of the burglary, she'll be passed on to the adult … Wait.*

Travis tried to think past the panic he felt.

"I don't panic. I ain't never panicked in my life."

He gritted his teeth and thought hard.

*Don't panic. You're okay. Get rid of the blade first chance you get and no one will be the wiser.*

"Just get rid of the blade girl. No blade, no trouble. You'll finish up your time and you'll be out, with nothin' on your record. Juve records will be sealed and expunged. You'll be free and no record."

*"Are you sure about that?"* whispered that other voice sibilantly. *"You know they have it in for you. You're black, a MIN-OR-IT-Y. You don't have rights, you have the MAN telling*

*you what to do all day long. You're a WO-MAN; you don't count half as much as a man. Just think of all the stupidity that we have to put up with. WE can take CONTROL of our lives. The first thing to do is take care of the bitches that are making your life miserable. Just take it and catch each one alone. Your blade will scare them. You won't have to take a beating ever again."*

"No, you don't want to do that. It'll just lead to more hate and more pain. You know that. You KNOW that."

The view on the curved wall shifted back to the bed, and shook as the girl got back into it, palming the surgical blade in her left hand. The view spun to center on the door as another clatter sounded. The door swung open as the orderly pushed in a wheeled cart which held a sandwich and a glass of water.

"Here you go, girl. Ham, cheese, and some water to wash it down. You'll be released today. Looks like the most you got was some good bruises. You got off lucky."

The heavy-set nurse continued to talk about the day, and the other inmates in the infirmary, while the view followed her so intently that Travis thought the nurse would catch on how nervous the girl was.

INTERESTING SITUATION, ISN'T IT? scrolled in bright orange across the view, temporarily blocking the display.

"Dammit! Get out of the way!" Travis snapped at the letters. "I gotta see what's going on."

The letters grew to cover the entire screen, mocking his demand. Then they faded, giving him a view of her pulling her prison scrubs back on. The nurse held out a clipboard as she walked to the small desk at the door of the infirmary. She signed her name, then set the clipboard back down on the desk, while the nurse buzzed her through the door back into the general population.

Travis watched her progress to the bedroom, the sullen eyes of the other juvenile inmates as she walked, head low, shoulders hunched, as she avoided the others. The guards made perfunctory nods at her as she padded through the corridors. He felt her anxiety as she got closer to her own room. The last few yards she fought not to run. She reached for the door, opening, closing. A sob escaped him, and her, as the girl sat down on the edge of the bed. The little blue dresser with the white alarm clock were no comfort. The blade appeared in her left hand. The view centered on that image for a full minute. Both Travis and the other voice remained silent. Travis wanted her to think it through and toss the blade, but it felt like he was talking to an addict with a "fix" in her hand. No matter how much she wanted to throw it away, she couldn't open her hand.

The hands slid the top drawer open. Socks, t-shirts, bras, and panties lay in neat rows left to right. The left hand opened, then tore the paper of the blade, which gleamed a polished silver under the fluorescent lighting. a pair of blue socks were grabbed by the right, and the blade thrust into them, and put at the far back of the drawer. The socks and the other articles were straightened, then the drawer closed.

The view changed to the corner the small desk there. The desk was built into the wall, with a small round stool that swung out for sitting. The wall screen moved closer to the desk, then shifted as the girl sat down. The screen leaned towards the desk and went dark. A moment later, faint shudders vibrated through the room as a choked sob emanated from the screen.

*Oh man, she is taking this all way too hard. She'll make herself sick with all this. There's got to be something I can do — or convince her to do.*

THAT'S THE JOB, JIMINY. OH, SORRY ... TRAVIS-INY.

The letters looked like a kid's scribble, in bright red.

"So what's the deal with that other voice? That guy sucks, you know! He's trying to get her to attack those thugs one at a time with that blade! What're you gonna do to stop her?! She'll screw her life up if she—"

The letters suddenly loomed from the floor up the curved wall to meet at the top of the hemispherical room. The black was so intense it made the room seem to squeeze his body like a vise.

I WILL DO NOTHING, JIMINY. THAT'S MY JOB. YOU'RE HERE TO DO YOURS, AND I CAN'T HELP YOU, OTHER THAN HOW I HAVE DONE SO, TO BREAK YOU INTO YOUR JOB. I AM NOT HERE TO JUMP AT YOUR COMMAND. YOU, TRAVIS JEFFTOWN HOAD, ARE HERE TO DO IT.

# 6

T RAVIS FOUND HIMSELF CRINGING AWAY FROM THE LETTERS. They seemed to pound down on him in with each word that they formed. It left him shaken to the core.

*What is this I've gotten into? It is like some monster in the closet. Kimmy, dear god I need you right now.*

SHE HAS HER LIFE THAT MUST GO ON. YOU. ARE. DEAD. SUCK IT UP, BUTTERCUP, AND DO. THE. JOB.

The letters had that impatient feel like when he first got here. Impatient and ... worried?

Travis shook his head as the soft hiccupping sobs barely sounded through the room, but he felt each one like an ache in his heart.

*If she's crying, she's not certain it will work? I don't know, but I hope that's right. I don't want her to use that thing and, if she's too scared, then we can dodge that bullet.*

As if on cue, the soft, hissing voice started up again.

*"Yes, you are weak, and helpless, you stupid little girl. They're going to come for you, and you can't stop it from happening. They will find you, trap you, and kick the ever-loving shit out of you, because you wouldn't mule for them. Your only hope is that blade, unless, of course, you want to fix it forever."*

*Fix it forever?*

*"All you have to do is cut yourself, let it flow out, and no one can ever hurt you again."*

The voice hissed with a poison-sweet purr. Sympathy, laced with venom, each word deepening her despair.

*"It isn't so hard. It's not the end — it's a transition. One from this world to the next. You can be free of this miserable, beat-down existence. So why not end it now, and move on to the next?"*

"NO! No no no no! You aren't that! You don't want to do that!"

Travis found himself screaming at the wall as hands clasped and unclasped at the bottom edge. Panic filled him.

*How could you think that? Dying's not an answer! If I could get hold of that miserable sonuvabitch, I'd beat him into a bloody pulp!*

Travis clenched and unclenched his hands around the poles as he stood on the platform. His hands ached to have that smarmy asshole's neck between them. He'd give it a—

Movement on the screen caught his attention. The girl had stood up, and moved to the bed. She threw herself forward, her face landing against the pale blue pillow. The view went black as she buried her face in the pillow and began screaming. The rage resonated within Travis, burning his confusion and panic away.

*Girl's a fighter. We got a chance to turn this around.*

It seemed odd to Travis that her getting mad would make him optimistic, but he accepted it as true. Anger is not a place where a person tries to kill themselves.

*If she's mad, then that slimy asshat can't get her to cut herself up. Crud, but what about killing? That's too easy to do mad. There's gotta be a middle way. When the heck did I get so thoughtful? This ain't me. I'm the walk–up–and–throw–punches kind of guy.*

YOU WERE THAT KIND OF GUY. the letters marched across the dark wall. NOW YOU'RE DEAD. YOUR OLD LIFE IS NOT THIS EXISTENCE.

It was true. As much as Travis was caught up in all the tension and drama of this girl's life, he kept hanging onto his own memories as they slowly lost the passion that they had once engendered in him. The realization raised a flutter of anxiety.

*I don't want to forget, I don't want to lose all that Kimmy gave me.*

MELODRAMATIC MUCH?

The words displayed right to left. The mocking hues of pink and yellow drew a flash of anger and despair from somewhere deep inside him.

"I ain't gonna forget. And I ain't gonna quit feelin' them, you piece o' crap! They're mine! You can't take 'em from me! That's MY LIFE! It's MINE!" Travis screamed at the wall.

He heard an answering scream of muffled rage from the girl as the hiccupping sobs shifted to a building anger.

The other voice became clear as Travis quit his rant.

*"That's it. You can do something about them. The blade will make them stop hurting you. You should be mad. They're trying to CONTROL you. No one controls you. You are your own boss … your own woman. Show them what it means to cross you. They'll never do it again if you stick them with that blade."*

143

*Oh crapola. Me getting mad got her mad and that slimeball took advantage.*

Travis watched as the top drawer of the low dresser was opened again, and the socks with the blade hidden in them was pulled from its back.

"No one will give me shit like that again. No one's gonna a lay a han' on me if I don't want 'em to."

The venom with which she spat the words chilled Travis to the core. He could feel her hate and resolve start to solidify. If he didn't find a way to change it, there wouldn't be a future.

"Listen to me, please. This anger ain't gonna work. You're too mad. You're lettin' that guy rile you up so you don't think. He doesn't want you to think. That's how he works."

*I feel like a shoulder angel facing off a shoulder devil.*

GOT IT IN ONE, T. YOU ARE AND HE IS. the letters spelled out in bright neon blue floor to ceiling, surrounded by gold stars with "attaboy" written on them.

Sheer surprise stopped Travis voice.

*A shoulder angel? Like in that animated movie?*

EXACTOMUNDO, the letters printed in block three-D in white and ivory. Somehow they felt pleased and mocking at the same time.

The feeling had Travis gritting his teeth in irritation.

*Something about that screen makes me really pissed off. How does it know to do that?*

I PAY ATTENTION TO HOW YOU ANSWER, AND YOUR MOOD, JUST LIKE ANYONE WITH A SMIDGEN OF SENSE WOULD DO.

The letters had the mocking tilt as they marched in day-glow orange across the view, blurring Travis vision of what was happening with the socks.

"Get outta the way!" he screamed at the letters.

They stopped for a moment, then seemed to smirk as they slowly faded away.

The girl had pulled the blade out of the socks and was now turning it over in her hand a few times. It was like she saw something there beyond just the knife.

Travis closed his eyes and listened for the other voice. He *knew* it would be saying something right now.

*That's it: a little tape, and some padding to set it between your fingers, and a slap will open their throats, one at a time … easy as slicing cherry pie.*

*Oh god, please no. Wait, why am I so … oh yeah, the feedback the sign talked about.*

The link between his reaction and what was on the wall had him torn. He knew rationally that the girl was trying to find a way out of a bad situation, but the method was going to get her killed. Using a blade meant you were going to have to kill the person. In here, a blade would not just scare them off; it would make them decide to kill her right then and there. No excuses. No mercy. No more shoulder angel job.

There came a sense of mocking irritation from the screen, then letters in bright red rolled up from the bottom of the screen.

THROWING IN THE TOWEL ALREADY, JIMINY?

"I ain't throwin' nothin! I ain't gonna quit! Not now! Not ever! You hear me, you sonuvabitch! Never!"

His anger started pushing him more and more. Travis wanted to rage at the screen, and at the voice. Something made him continue to grip both of the embedded ski poles. That was a good thing, as a sudden, vicious whipping lurch nearly catapulted him into the wall. He stayed on the platform, more scared than angry now.

The girl, he felt, was also having second thoughts.

*I hope I can get through this time.*

# 7

W ITH THAT THOUGHT IN HIS MIND, Travis focused on the girl, on the situation. If he didn't reach her, even a little, it could really be 'game over'.

"Hey, I know you're upset, and things don't feel like they'll get better. You gotta understand something. You will see hard days, and you'll see good days. These are part of them hard days. If you keep on goin' this way, with that blade, you're gonna create more hard days — worse days than you can imagine. They'll treat you like an adult, and throw you in with the real hard cases. This ain't close to what's waitin' in real prison. You know that. It ain't too late. Just throw that blade away. It's nothin' but trouble and big-time prison if you keep it."

*"Put it away for now; no one will find it in those socks. Bed checks never look at socks. You're free and clear. If you're scared, I*

147

*understand completely. Not everyone has the guts to stand up for themselves. You'll be just another loser bitch who gets told to fuck prison guards to get things smuggled in. Of course that's all you're good for, obviously. If you wanted to take charge of your life, you'd be scoring some tape and a little bit of plastic to help make a handle,"* the voice whispered with poisonous sympathy.

The sullen anger at the voice's words rippled along Travis' skin like an icy, slimy hand. Fear was a cold chill up his back. He saw her put the blade back into the socks, and the socks back into the dresser. She lay down on the bed.

Travis saw the ceiling, where some staples still held torn bits of colored paper. The view remained on the ceiling as a sense of despair settled through Travis.

*What do I do? How do I get her to listen? She's going to get killed.*

He took deep breaths, and willed himself to calm down.

Travis focused on regular breathing, and realized for the first time that he hadn't been breathing at all, except for when he was shouting at the other voice.

*I am dead. I knew it before, but it keeps surprising me how weird things feel when I think about them. I need to keep her from dying. But how? I can't get her to listen. She doesn't want to. That creep has got her convinced that blade is the answer to everything.*

*How do I change that?*

He spent the rest of the day observing the life of a teenage girl — something which Travis had no desire to watch, or take part of. Instead, he focused on thoughts in his own head, trying to puzzle out how to get through to her before something that couldn't be changed happened.

*There has to be a way. Why can't I figure out a way to convince her?*

YOU KNOW YOU'RE CUTE WHEN YOU BROOD LIKE THAT. IT MAKES ME THINK YOU MIGHT ACTUALLY HAVE POTENTIAL, TRAVIS. NOT THAT YOU'VE SHOWN ANY, TO BE TRUTHFUL.

The tan letters seemed to actually contain a little sympathy, which made Travis suspicious.

WOULD I REALLY TRY TO MESS WITH YOU, OR INFLUENCE YOU? I WOULD LOSE MY JOB IF I DID THAT. ALL I AM IS JUST AN INFORMATION DEVICE. WITH ATTITUDE. SO YOU PAY ATTENTION.

*Yeah right, and I'm —*

DO YOU REALLY WANT TO FINISH THAT THOUGHT? REMEMBER THE THONG BIKINI.

The letters were a glaring white, with bikini tops and bottoms floating around the words as they rolled down from the top of the dome. The mocking warning got Travis' attention and he shut up.

"So got anything about this situation you can share without breaking any rules, Or do I gotta guess that too?"

*Maybe there's a way to get information. Maybe it's how I ask it?*

Letters in green, yellow, and blue popped onto the screen in haphazard order.

ASK AWAY, BUT I WILL WARN YOU THAT THE ONLY REAL ANSWER IS ONE YOU FIND. DON'T SAY I DIDN'T WARN YOU.

An honest-to-Smiley Face formed on the screen. Travis thought it was the creepiest thing he'd ever seen. It made him think of a serial killer toying with their chosen target.

MELODRAMATIC MUCH? it mocked with orange letters popping up and disappearing.

"That's just creepy, and you know it," Travis snarled at the screen, which remained dark.

OH MY, ACTUAL BANTER RATHER THAN SCREAMING FITS AND ANGRY SHOUTS? WHAT ARE WE COMING TO? DETENTE?

"De-*what*? Never mind. I have a question. You can answer questions, right?"

The letters took a coy, fuzzy pink texture as they appeared on the screen.

I CAN ... WITHIN LIMITS OF COURSE.

*We're getting somewhere.*

"So what are the limits?"

THE INFORMATION CAN'T FORCE YOU TO CHANGE YOUR ACTIONS. I AM NOT ALLOWED TO LIE OR INFLUENCE YOU IN ANY WAY.

"So if I asked for history about this girl, you can give it?"

POINT FOR YOU. YES I CAN, AND WILL GIVE ANY RELEVANT HISTORY WHEN ASKED.

The black letters outlined in orange had extra space between them, almost like they were saying something themselves, but Travis couldn't figure if it meant anything or not.

"What about asking things like, uh ... about the other guy?"

*Anything I can learn might help figuring out what his angle is, and how I could catch trouble before it got started.*

UH UH. NO NO NOOOO . . . NO CAN DO, KEMOSABE. INFORMATION LIKE THAT INFLUENCES DECISIONS. INFLUENCE IS A NO-NO. SAME THING FOR THE OTHER GUY.

"So the other guy can't use you to, uh ..."

Travis stopped talking and thought hard about what he'd heard so far.

"Wait a sec. You can tell me about the girl's history, but won't that influence me?"

POINT FOR YOU. showed up in thin gold letters, along with a different looking "attaboy" — a shiny silver one that reminded Travis of a sticker his first-grade teacher gave out to students that got a perfect score on their tests.

SINCE IT'S HISTORY, IT'S NOT SOMETHING THAT CAN BE INFLUENCED. IT CAN BE LEARNED FROM. THAT'S YOUR JOB — AT LEAST PART OF IT: TO LEARN. IF IT HAPPENS TO INFLUENCE YOUR DECISION, THEN YOU'VE LEARNED FROM THE PAST, NOT FROM ME.

It made Travis head hurt a little. That it could — and would — talk about the past, and yet not talk about now and other possible things going on.

*That seems a weird place to draw a line about what's proper and what ain't.*

I DON'T MAKE THE RULES, I JUST ABIDE BY THEM. floated down the wall from the ceiling in block white letters.

"Ya don't mind screwin' around either, do ya?" Travis grumbled.

PERISH THE THOUGHT came the dark blue letters from right to left. I MAY BE A LITTLE MISCHIEVOUS, BUT I AM THE SOUL OF THE WORK ETHIC. EVERYTHING FOR A REASON AND EVERYTHING IN IT'S PROPER TIME AND PLACE.

"Okay, so what got her here? I saw the botched burglary. What made her do it?" Travis felt this was important.

OH, IT IS IMPORTANT, AND IT IS HISTORY, SO SIT DOWN AND I'LL LAY THE WORD UPON YOUR EARS, JIMINY.

The letters had that mocking attitude again, and the bright neon orange letters bursting on the wall screen made Travis eyes ache to look at them. The letters scrolled right to left in a baby-powder blue.

# 8

ONCE UPON A TIME, A LITTLE GIRL WAS BORN TO A WHORE MOTHER AND A DRUG-ADDLED GANG-BANGER FATHER. THIS LITTLE GIRL GREW UP IN A HOUSE WHERE NEITHER PARENT LOOKED AFTER HER, AND ONLY HER DRUNKEN GRANDMOTHER EVER PAID HER ANY ATTENTION BEYOND THE OCCASIONAL SNARL AND BACKHAND FROM THE GIRLS PARENTS. IT WAS SO, SO SAD.

THE LITTLE GIRL WENT TO SCHOOL, WITH THE OTHER HARD-LUCK CHILDREN FROM THE DESPERATELY POOR SECTION OF TOWN, AND FOUND THAT THE "NORMAL" KIDS HAD MORE EVERYTHING THAN SHE DID. HER JUVENILE DELINQUENT FRIENDS SHOWED HER HOW EASY IT WAS TO GET "NORMAL" KIDS MONEY FROM THEM, BUT SHE DIDN'T LIKE BEATING PEOPLE UP. INSTEAD, SHE FOUND SHE LIKED

LEARNING THINGS. THIS MADE HER STAY AFTER SCHOOL AND ASK QUESTIONS ABOUT CLASSES.

ONE DAY, THE GIRLS PARENTS MOVED OUT, LEAVING HER BEHIND. SHE WAS A TEENAGER, AND DIDNT HAVE ANY WAY TO SUPPORT HERSELF. SHE WAS ALL ALONE — THE POOR, POOR THING. SO, SHE FOUND OUT THAT STEALING WAS THE ONLY WAY TO GET FOOD. SHE TOOK FROM THE SUPERMARKET, STUFFING SNACKS IN HER PANTS, AND WADDLING OUT OF THE STORE. STEALING MONEY WAS EASIER, AND HER FRIENDS SHOWED HER HOW TO SNEAK INTO A HOUSE, TEASE THE WINDOW OPEN, AND TAKE VALUABLE THINGS TO SELL TO FENCES OR PAWN SHOPS. OH, SHE WAS CAREFUL TO CASE A PLACE FIRST, JUST LIKE THE BIG KIDS TAUGHT HER. THAT WAY SHE COULD PICK THE BEST TIME TO BURGLE A RESIDENCE. IT WAS EASY. A LITTLE BIT HERE, A LITTLE BIT THERE, WAS GOOD ENOUGH FOR HER — BUT NOT HER NEW FRIENDS, WHO WANTED MORE. SO OUR LARCENOUS LITTLE HEROINE TOOK LARGER AND LARGER RISKS TO SATISFY HER "FRIENDS". "Friends" was spelled out in dark red block letters.

SOME TIME LATER, THE FRIENDS DECIDED THAT BURGLING A HOUSE WASN'T GOOD ENOUGH. THEY FELT READY FOR SOMETHING ... MORE. TO KEEP HER FRIENDS HAPPY, SHE JOINED IN. HER FRIEND, CASEY, DROVE TO THE LIQUOR STORE THEY'D CASED. OUR HEROINE WAS THE "NEW KID". SO SHE WAS CHOSEN TO BE THE FIRST IN THROUGH THE DOOR. SHE HAD PICKED UP A CEMENT BLOCK FROM A WORK SITE A FEW DAYS AGO FOR JUST SUCH AN OPPORTUNITY. SHE THREW THE BLOCK HARD AT THE WINDOW, AND SMASHED IT. A SECOND THROW CARRIED AWAY ENOUGH GLASS FOR HER TO WIGGLE IN AND START TO SEARCH FOR ANYTHING VALUABLE.

SHE ROLLED OVER THE COUNTER, AND STARTED THROWING CIGARETTE CARTONS BACK OUTSIDE FOR HER FRIENDS TO PICK UP. THE CASH REGISTER WAS LOCKED. SHE COULDN'T PRY IT OPEN. ABOUT THIS TIME, SHE HEARD THE CAR REV. ITS TIRES SQUEALED AND SHE WAS LEFT IN THE STORE, FROZEN BY HER "FRIENDS" SUDDEN DISAPPEARANCE. SUDDENLY, A COP FLASHED A LIGHT INTO THE DARK STORE. BEFORE HE COULD CALL OUT, SHE THREW A METAL CAN AT THE OFFICER, CATCHING HIM IN THE SIDE OF THE HEAD. HE DROPPED TO THE GROUND. AS SHE LOOKED FOR AN ESCAPE, THE SECOND OFFICER SPOTTED HER IN THE STORE, AND FIRED A TASER GUN. SHE WAS SENTENCED TO SERVE A YEAR IN JUVENILE DETENTION FOR ASSAULTING AN OFFICER.

OH, THE POOR, POOR LITTLE POOR BITCH FROM GANG-BANGERS. WHO WOULD HAVE THOUGHT SHE'D SINK SO LOW? IS THERE NO SHAME IN THE WORLD ANYMORE? WHY, IT'S HARD TO BELIEVE THAT ANY UPRIGHT MEN AND WOMEN ACTUALLY EXIST.

The words had shifted slowly from an innocent-feeling white as the story scrolled across the wall to a dark, dark red as the story wound down. Travis' skin crawled as the story unfolded. He felt the weight and truth behind every word as he read them and thought about the girl. The words glossed things, but the feelings that he got from the girl were nothing like he'd ever experienced. He didn't retch at the emotional overload, but he wanted to.

*Her life is so different from mine, how do I help her? How did she survive all of the abuse without going bugnuts? Maybe that's why she's here, but I haven't seen anything crazy. Desperate, yeah. Crazy, no. How do I go about fixing something like this? She already got beat down because I couldn't control my temper, and made her lose control. Number one: think calm thoughts. Number two: think around the problem, if I can.*

That sense of something in his world changing crawled over his skin once more, like a leech looking for a good place to latch on.

*I never felt this smart before. Is this come kind of requisite for the job, that I get smarter? Why? It doesn't make sense.*

He glanced over at the screen, half-expecting some snark about his thoughts, but the wall remained blank … ominously so.

STILL WAITING FOR THE SNARKY COMMENT, JIMINY? WELL, IT'S NOT GOING TO HAPPEN THE WAY YOU THINK. the letters marched across the wall, floor to domed ceiling in bright, discordant orange.

The whole room seemed to darken as the letters faded, dissipating into an orange mist that sucked light like a hole into itself, giving a blood-like tint to the air.

*This is seriously creepy. It's like he's upping his game. I know the stakes are big, but how big is this supposed to go?*

Travis wiped his clammy hands on his work shirt, then used both hands to cover his nose and lips.

*Can I do this? This girl's seriously screwed up, and I have no real clue how to talk to a kid; I never raised any. And my life wasn't what anyone would call proper upbringing: getting ignored or beat for talking. It's a wonder that I didn't go postal. Maybe the bullying was the outlet valve or something.*

The teal letters slipped mockingly across the wall.

GOING FOR ANOTHER LITTLE SELF-EXAMINATION, JIMINY? OH, SO SAD, TOO BAD. THE BIG FAT BOY BECAME A BIG FAT MAN WITH NO DREAMS. ALL THIS WORRY FOR HER IS ACTUALLY A PITY PARTY FOR YOURSELF, ISN'T IT NOW, JIMINY?

Travis' blood did a slow boil. He'd a bellyful of snark from that screen. Whatever it was, he wanted to punch its face in and kick it around the yard; twice, just to give it a proper payback.

His hands clenched hard enough that his wrists ached. A growl echoed through the chamber, throwing a dash of cold water on his emotions.

*Every time. If I get mad, it spills over on her. That smart mouth said it went both ways, so could my mood be what she's feeling. Has to be. So, if that's true, then there's an early warning about her mood, maybe her thoughts? That last is a reach. Go with just mood. Why does that make me think we're mood rings for each other?*

POINT FOR YOU, JIMINY.

The words slid downward in a dark mauve and disappeared at the bottom of the wall.

Travis started to retort, but movement on the front screen caught his attention. The other girl was rapidly throwing things back in her chest of drawers, her face pale.

From out in the hall came a loud voice.

"Inspection! Drop what you're doing and up against the wall! We're doing an inspection! Hurry it up, ladies! Inspection! Get your fluffy asses out of your rooms and against the wall by the doors! Hands at your sides! No speaking unless spoken to! You got ten seconds to line up! Nine, eight, …"

# 9

THE WALL AND THE FLOOR TILTED CRAZILY as the girl sprang up, shoved the drawer closed, and walked out to stand by the door. Just after the guard finished counting, her roommate darted from down the hall to stand next to her.

"Bell, you're late!" bellowed the guard. "We're going to do you first! Harris, take Ms. Bell back in the room and have her empty her closet and dresser on the bed. Go through everything! If there's a hair out of place, I want it written up!"

Her eyes followed Bell back into the room, then seemed to flick to Travis, to the girl, and bore right through her.

*Oh shit, this lady's a terror! I really don't want to —*

"Hey, nothing to fear. Come on, calm down. Her job is to get in your grill and shake you up. Don't let it get to you."

Travis could feel her body start to relax a little.

*"Nothing to fear, he says. I told you to hide that blade better. They're going to ask for you next, and guess what they'll find when they go through your socks?"* the voice whispered from the walls.

Travis could feel her tense up.

"SHADDUP!"

Travis blinked. The voice shut up.

Silence reigned for a few moments.

*Who said that? Was it me? Was it her? I can't be certain. Oh, god, do we got another one in here?*

Travis' own confusion seemed to make her tense up again. This time he could feel it and slowed his own breathing, calming himself. He felt the girl start to relax. The guard walked heavy-footed to stand in front of her. The girl seemed to stare directly at the curved wall. Travis felt that desperate gaze like a tremendous weight that made it hard to think.

*That damn bastard might …*

Thought went to action.

"Listen to me. Listen. To. Me. Your fear is going to get you in deeper. The blade needs to go. Do you want this for yourself for the rest of your life? No. This is a chance to —" and the voice cut in, just like Travis thought it would.

*"Listen,"* came the silky, poisonous words. *"You don't want to be a loser all your life. The blade gets you cred, gets you Re-SPECT. No one will ever try to screw with you again. That blade is your ticket to a new life. You know how it is. No power, no respect, no LIFE. Loser. That's all you'll be. Skank. Ho'. A piece of meat for them 'bangers to pass around like a joint."*

Travis' room went cold, and the air became sharp like ozone after a lightning strike. His 'boss' was tense, only this time with self-hate. Her focus on the blade, and one of the guards seemed to notice that something about her had changed.

The head guard, with three stripes indicating a sergeant, strode purposely towards "the boss". She straightened her back, deliberately looming over "the boss" with her bulk.

"Somethin' got yer panties in a bunch, skel?"

"Look down, look down. We don't want any trouble right now. We just stay quiet, stay invisible, and we can dump that stupid blade first chance after inspection."

*Please god,* Travis prayed. *Please let her listen this one time.*

HE DOESN'T ANSWER HERE. THIS IS YOUR TEST, JIMINY.

The block three-D letters were vivid blood red against a black background. They loomed over him as they stretched from the floor, up the curved walls to the ceiling: the emptiness of oblivion made manifest.

Travis tried to pee himself, but being dead prevented that from happening. The fear tasted metallic in his mouth, like a live battery that had just zinged his tongue, and wasn't going to stop until his whole body shook. He scrabbled backwards on hands and feet, not realizing he'd fallen. His only objective was to get away from the words that made his soul — made *him* — shiver in terror.

WHAT'S THE MATTER, JIMINY? THE BIG, BAD LETTERS SCARE YOU AND YOU FALL DOWN?

The letters spread and blended together, making the wall seem to drip blood down to the floor, where it rippled red and black, surrounding Travis with lurid color. There was nowhere for him to go. He was surrounded by the red and black.

Travis glanced wildly around as the room began to fade around him. A frantic glance caught movement. He saw the guard, looming, like the black and red around him, over his view.

"Answer me, skel! What's got you scared? Afraid I'm gonna find something?" The guard lowered her face to the girl's. "Answer me."

Travis watched, and felt, as "the boss" began to lose it.

The view lowered as her head tilted down. The floor lurched as before, but this time Travis leaned back, fighting to remain level. The platform surprisingly responded to his desire, and rotated as if on gimbals, remaining level as the floor remained angled. The ominous red and black still pulsed right at the edge of the level section of floor, slowly creeping towards him. It didn't hold the overwhelming terror as it had earlier. Travis had quit giving it attention, and it had lost its ability to control him.

*Okay, that's good to know: If I don't let it get to me, all it can do is barf colors all over the place.*

POINT FOR YOU, JIMINY. rolled up in gold letters and bright yellow "attaboy" stickers.

Travis ignored them as he concentrated on mentally projecting calm at "the boss". It was hard. The guard was right up against her, crowding her mercilessly as she tried to break the girl down.

"Easy, easy. They can't touch you, or they would have already. What you have to do is relax. Since you're roomies with 'Bell', they're going to lean on you too, just to see if you break. That blade was the wrong thing to grab, and you know it now. We'll dump it tomorrow. Tonight, just relax. Don't look up; don't break down. You've already shown you're tough enough to survive this. You're tough enough to change your life the way you want. Those girls can give you grief, but they can't make you do something you don't want to. You know the score and you can change. This life can be left at the door when you leave."

Travis could hear the other voice in the background as he soothed her agitation.

*"You'll be discovered! You get jumped for sure!"*

It continued shrilly, chiding her for being stupid and not hiding the blade better. But it was like water against a pier: a lot of movement and noise, but no real effect.

Travis could feel her relax as she lowered her eyes, and said quietly, "Still feeling the pain meds the nurse gave me today."

"The boss" looked back up at the guard, then straight ahead, calmly, her back against the cold cement wall.

The guard's chest swelled as she drew in a breath. It actually looked as if she was going to push the issue, but a noise caught her attention. She swiveled towards the offending sound.

"Ramierez! What the hell was that?!"

The guard stalked off towards the new subject of her attention. Both Travis and "the boss" breathed a very quiet sigh of relief, like a glass of clear, cold, fresh water.

*She did it. She hung in when she could've broken. For that matter, so did I. That means she listened? She did listen, right?*

POINT FOR YOU, JIMINY. SHE LISTENED.

The block gold letters glowed against what looked like black velvet, surrounded by small floating silver trophies. Each trophy had "I almost blew it" clearly printed in black block lettering.

CONGRATULATIONS ON SURVIVING THE FIRST TEST.

Sunlight poured through the screen like a benediction.

*I did it. I can do it again. You hear me? We can do it again.*

Travis thought the room rocked slightly in agreement. It was a bit of shared joy in the midst of fear. Travis knew the knife would disappear tomorrow.

AND TOMORROW'S ANOTHER DAY, JIMINY. WERE NOT FINISHED. NOT UNTIL, YOU KNOW, SHE IS. WHICH, SHOULD NOT BE FOR A LONG TIME, IF, YOU KEEP HER ON THE STRAIGHT AND NARROW.

"Whatta ya mean 'if'?!" Travis thumped his chest with a closed fist. "That girl deserves a break, and I wanna see her get it! I ain't quittin' until she gets one!"

POINT FOR YOU, JIMINY.

Travis thought he sensed a note of warm approval in the letters. He lifted his chin and glared at the screen, a sharp smile on his lips.

"Damn straight."

SKID STYLE

*One of the jobs I have worked at was a comic book store. In there, if you're an avid reader, you could get story overload. It was such a great place to work. All those comics, both old and new, had some tremendously awesome stories, and some that left your head wondering why someone ever wrote a story like that. Comics to me are a very necessary medium for getting new and controversial ideas out in a non-threatening format for people to read about, and ponder in a medium that is non-threatening. "Skid Style" came from reading comics, (of which there are at least six four-foot boxes full of them here) and using the idea of a relatively new hero trying to earn his chops.*

# SKID STYLE

C HARLIE 'SKID' MOORE sat on the edge of the warehouse roof, north of Pier 17 — one of the few areas in the dockyards that were still unloading containers for transport. Boston Harbor never stopped; it just slowed down in the evenings. Charlie fidgeted restlessly, impatient for something to happen, yet oddly comforted that nothing had.

*I'd have never thought I'd be here.*

Charlie had always been fast: fastest in his grade school, in middle school, and then in high school. There was talk of scholarships for college. Even though he was still a junior, recruiters had stopped by and talked to his folks. Then, a short while after the recruiting started, Charlie got *fast*.

It happened at a school crossing. Classes had just let out. Students were queuing to load up on buses. A line of primary students was crossing the street. As Charlie watched, a red sports car with a driver talking on a cellphone whizzed past him, and towards the line of children. He heard the car's tires screech as the driver realized, too late, that there were children in her path. Charlie's heart rose into his throat as he began to run.

*I'm not going to make it! Those kids are dead!*

The world blurred. Sharp images stretched and blended into a chaotic whirl of color. A loud roaring, like a jumbo jet taking off right next to him, assaulted his ears. An abrupt impact knocked the breath out of him.

His eyes cleared at the sudden stop, everything snapping into sharp focus. The red sports car spun wildly away, its right front side crumpled like cardboard, its right front tire blown and half off its rim. It skidded across the oncoming lanes and hit the curb, blowing both left tires. With a screech of grinding metal, the car ground to a stop on the sidewalk. The children were untouched; the driver had fractured ribs, whiplash, and a concussion. Charlie had bruises … and a new life.

Overnight, he went from promising athlete to something he'd barely ever thought about: superhero. He was no longer a candidate for a scholarship to college. Now, he was a metahuman. A person with power to change things. To stand up to those who used their power for terror and personal profit. Charlie — being the young, idealistic high-school student, and raised on morning cartoons — embraced his new life. Only, his new life came with a few unexpected bumps in the road.

There's an old acronym: 'TANSTAAFL', which means 'There Ain't No Such Thing As A Free Lunch'. In short, it means that no matter how great something seems, there is always some trouble that comes with it. In Charlie's case, his speed was amazing. In fact, he was so fast that his eyes couldn't keep up.

Above sixty miles an hour, Charlie's vision started to blur at around twenty yards, which was still enough time for him to react, but as he ran faster, the distance at which the blurring happened increased. It formed an increasingly narrow 'tunnel' ahead of him where his vision could make out detail. Any faster, and it got to the point he couldn't react quickly enough to something in his path.

The number of inadvertent crashes and near-misses got Charlie the nickname "Skid" in the Boston papers. He never took any permanent damage from the impacts — something about his body being more durable helped — but that didn't help what he ran into. Fortunately, there were no major incidents, and Charlie learned to keep his velocity down to avoid the 'tunnel vision'. He could run at supersonic speeds, but his eyes were still regular human, and still perceived images at roughly sixteen images per second.

This might seem like a lot, but in truth, much of the brain's attempts at following things, such as a ninety-mile-an-hour baseball, are as much estimation as actual tracking. After closing to a certain distance, the ball itself blurs out of focus due to its change of position. It was the same for Charlie.

As he ran, the sharpest part of his vision was straight ahead, and only for a distance. The faster he ran, the tighter his tunnel vision became, and things blurred out of focus further away from him.

*If I could only see stuff around me going fast, this'd be a whole lot more fun.*

\*　　\*　　\*

Charlie, true to comic book form, got his sister to sew him a bright red and blue uniform out of spandex and neoprene so that he could be seen better. He was so noticeable, that being visible caused some other, unique problems. People, especially those in the news business, and fanatics on both sides of the 'superhero' argument, were prone to following him around. It made it hard for him to enjoy just being himself for the sake of it.

*I wanted the hero life; I guess those guys come with it.*

He slowed to check traffic ahead of him before turning onto Congress Street. He would rather have taken a less-crowded road, but there weren't any that went through beyond Congress and the much more crowded Seaport Boulevard. As he crossed the bridge into the active harbor, he turned north, heading towards the docks proper.

*I'll start patrolling there. The scanner last night said there were a few robberies. Some missing crates and busted loading doors. I can check that.*

He angled off onto Belcher Street, heading towards the docks. His field of vision narrowed. His eyes started to have trouble registering things closest to him. The 'tunnel vision' continued to narrow as he accelerated.

*I really, really wish I could see better.*

\*     \*     \*

Skid turned off Belcher, then slowed and angled onto Collier. The street ran north, and fronted the warehouses that stored the cargo from the ships being serviced. The pace on the docks, and in the warehouses, was frantic. It looked to Charlie like an anthill that had been kicked open. Cranes moved cargo off the freighters in large pallets. Another freighter slid containers down a ramp to waiting eighteen-wheel tractor-trailer flatbeds. The line of trucks stretched over a quarter-mile, by his estimate.

Charlie looked forward just in time to avoid drifting into the curb at forty miles an hour. He over-corrected and moved into the oncoming lane, grunting as he planted his foot and shifted back into the proper lane.

*I gotta pay more attention. I can handle a wipeout, but not an oncoming car. Where is the turnoff to the dockyard?*

Charlie's mental question was answered a moment later as the road ended at a "T" intersection. He slowed then slewed right, skidding on the loose gravel, and straightened out, slowing to avoid a tumble, and approached the gate. The gate was a railroad crossing re-purposed for traffic control. It was currently down as the gate guard checked the papers on a Brown and yellow UPS truck.

The outbound lane had a tractor trailer slowly moving forward to leave the docks. At his speed, Charlie would be there before the truck could clear the gate and, with four others behind it, there was no way to use the oncoming lane to bypass the guard. 'Skid' slowed as he approached the gate, raising his hand to his bright blue pullover mask to make certain it was still in place. The heavyset gate guard stopped talking as the bright red-and-blue stocky superhero trotted up to the gate.

"Whatta ya want, uh, kid? I'm kinda busy here", the guard said with a surprisingly soft voice.

Charlie took a moment to realize that the guard was a woman. He blushed crimson underneath his mask as he tried to sound authoritative.

"Sorry, ma'am. I'd heard that some stuff was stolen last night. I came by to look the, uh, scene over and see if there is something that, umm, would help find the crooks."

He tried to puff his chest out, and got the mental image of a cartoon mouse trying to look tough while facing a cat.

The man that the guard was talking to had also turned to look over at Skid, then turned back to the guard with a small chuckle, making Charlie blush even redder underneath the mask.

"I suppose I could let you look around. Heck, seeing you prowling might make them guys with sticky fingers decide not to try anything if a costume's poking around." She pressed a button, raising the gate, then waved her clipboard at Skid. "G'wan through. Place that got hit's on the north side up there."

Charlie nodded, then trotted around the van, accelerating back to a somewhat cautious thirty miles an hour. He slowed again as he dodged a swarm of fork lifts moving pallets of crates and boxes to the white concrete warehouse on his left. The traffic was incessant, with two men shouting orders to the stream of workers and equipment coming from a docked freighter. The noise was near deafening as Skid dodged swiftly, and awkwardly between the moving vehicles and people.

*    *    *

He stumbled over a generator cable, caught his balance, then was in the clear once again, until a few docks later when he repeated the process. Four minutes, and a good deal of dodging later, Charlie came to the north end of the dockyard. This was where the burglaries had happened.

Charlie slowed to a stop. The docks here were narrower than at the south end, and older. Years of weather had turned the wooden planking grey. Cement had been poured next to the planks, widening the dock area outwards to hold the larger loading equipment. The warehouses abutted the edge of the docks. Their wood and red-brick single-story construction looked to Charlie like huge turtles that came ashore and died in place.

The break-in had happened on the dock side of the northernmost building. That yellow police tape still hung on the front door and huge loading dock next to it was a big clue.

Charlie took a long look at the building as the sun baked the asphalt and concrete. The air carried the mixed scents of salt water and decaying fish to his nostrils. He looked towards the docks, which was no help.

The last two piers had no ships, and no workers around to talk to. He turned to look back south. The nearest potential witness was about a hundred yards away, and there were a couple hundred more servicing a pair of freighters.

Charlie watched the cranes on the pier move large pallets of crates. The grey, blue, and yellow forklifts picked up smaller pallets off the large pallet and, like ants in a line, rolled back towards the warehouses to drop off their cargo.

He turned back towards the south. The sunlight glinting off the forklifts scuttling back and forth was mesmerizing.

Charlie blinked, then sighed, "What do I do now?"

Night settled down over the dockyard. While the sounds of traffic had slowly dissipated, the cacophony of the cranes and workers remained at full roar. The sounds carried faintly to Charlie, who had moved to the end of the old, weather-worn pier to watch for thieves coming back to break into the warehouse.

*They gotta return to the scene of the crime. This place is too easy not to pick over.*

Charlie crossed his fingers, hoping he was right. All those comics and mysteries he loved so much said that bad guys always came back for more.

*I just have to wait, and I'll catch them red-handed.*

He settled in for a night of watching, only to find out the rule that every cop who had ever been on a stakeout figured out: The crooks will never appear when you're awake or ready — if they show at all.

This waiting on a stakeout was a new experience — and a boring one. He kept himself awake by running down to the first active dock, then back again to the end of the old pier, with the predictable results of letting people know he was around.

It was eleven-thirty at night when a heavy-set figure drove up in a dark car. The vehicle's lights were out as it purred to a stop next to the warehouse.

*This has got to be it!* Charlie thought excitedly. It was just like the comics. The crooks came back for more!

He didn't wait, but dashed up to the car, shouting "Freeze! You're under arrest!"

The car's floodlight mounted on the right side of the car came on immediately and spun to illuminate him.

Charlie blinked in the light as a voice said, "Jesus Christ! What the hell are you doing, kid! Trying ta give me a heart attack?!"

The voice was familiar somehow, but Charlie decided to ignore it and confront them like the hero he was supposed to be.

Skid ran quickly to the driver-side door and gave it a hard yank. The interior light came on to illuminate the gate guard, sitting in the driver's seat. Her face was pale in the glare of the harsh mercury lighting from the parking lot lamps. Charlie felt his cheeks flush in embarrassment.

"Uh, sorry. I didn't think … I just didn't think."

The stammered apology seemed to calm the guard, who managed a thin smile. She shifted in her seat. The door clicked as she pulled the inner lever and opened it, shifting her heavyset bulk out through the doorway and into the muggy night air.

"I understand. It's no big deal. I scared myself on my first evening doing guard work." She paused a moment, then took a breath as she seemed to gather her thoughts. "It was six years ago I got hired. I'd just gotten out of college with a degree in Biology, only to find no one wanted a biologist without a masters, or a doctorate. I jumped on the job. The lead out here gave me the route to drive, what to check, and where to stamp the clock to prove I covered my route."

Her eyes lit up with the remembered first night. "One thing that they forgot to tell me was that Pier Eight was a twenty-four-hour pickup for priority loads. I drove past the gate, and found it open. At night, all the gates are supposed to be locked. This one was wide open and a pickup was sitting just inside. People were scurrying around flashing lights at the crates, then loading them onto the pickup. There were seven of them and just me with a Maglite and walkie-talkie."

"I called it in quietly, and you know what my lead said?" She chuckled. "He said 'go check it out, rookie. Oh, and don't get shot' — which didn't help my paranoia at all. I walked in and announced myself, at which point there were a couple of screams. The guys dropped the small crate they were moving and seven flashlights swiveled onto me. 'Jesus ma'am! What the hell are you giving us a heart attack for!? We called it in and I've got the papers for the pick up right here."

"I could hear frigging laughing coming over the walkie. I'd been so tense I'd held the transmit button on. My lead had set me up." She chuckled again, then turned what was supposed to be a stern face at Skid, but her smile ruined the whole stern thing.

He found himself grinning at the story. "So, did you get him back?" he asked her.

The guard, whose name was "Menendez", according to her name badge just above her left chest pocket, smiled, and shook her head.

"No, it doesn't work that way. Though, I do seem to remember someone replaced his sugar packets with salt once."

Skid chuckled, then looked around the parking lot again.

"Is this you trying to tell me that I'm wasting my time?"

*   *   *

Ms. Menendez stepped closer to Skid, who stood a whole head taller.

"Yeah, I suppose you could take it like that." She shrugged, then adjusted her jacket and web belt. "I'm sure you might think crooks would come back to the scene of the crime to rob it again, since it was so easy the first time. Trust me. They're going to go look elsewhere. Too much attention down here for them to be comfortable with a second try. You're not inconspicuous in that costume. A super like yourself is bad news for bad guys. Since you've decided to stake this place out, they won't come back. There's plenty of other docks to lift stuff from."

Skid felt his heart sink a little. He'd hoped to catch them in the act here. He looked around the parking lot and back to the warehouse once more.

"I guess you might be right. Maybe they know I'm out here looking for trouble."

He looked at Ms. Menendez, who bent over and slowly maneuvered herself back into her car. She put her seat belt back on and closed the door. The car started with a soft roar.

She smiled at Skid, then said, "I know it ain't easy bein' a super. Just let me say I like you out here. It makes my job a little easier."

"I think I'll stick around then. See what happens. I'm fast enough to cover the whole yard."

Ms. Menendez chuckled. "Yeah, you do that."

Skid grinned, then sped off to the south, and made a quick stop-and-go circuit of the quiet docks short of the new modern cement piers. He took a quick look around, then sped off the dock to the pile of crates waiting for pickup in the morning. A quick glance showed no activity at the near end. He carefully gauged the distance for a few moments, then looked around for any potential witnesses.

His speed — his actual top speed — was in the Mach numbers. He had been tested on a treadmill ... and burned it out with little effort. Its top listed speed, before it tore itself apart and nearly launched him into a wall, was three hundred and fifty miles an hour. That had been the only test Charlie did, despite the scientists repeated entreaties to "come back for more tests".

*You'd think once was enough. It sure was for me.* He shook his arms and legs, then looked around. *Let's try a quick start and stop. I don't think I can mess anything up here.* He crouched down, then *accelerated*.

With his first step, the world blurred around him. He started decelerating immediately, skidding to a stop way down near the end of the pier. Wood chips and chunks bounded past him, bouncing along the pier, until they disappeared off the end, falling with tiny splashes into the water. Charlie looked down the last ten feet to the end of the pier, and its flimsy wooden fence. From there, it was a good twenty feet to the rocky water.

*I wonder if I'd skip across the water at that speed?*

He heard a gasp behind him and turned.

\*     \*     \*

His braking had torn huge chunks and splinters from the wooden pier. It looked like someone had dragged a crane scoop along the entire length of the wood. Some of the crates had been spun sideways by the shockwave of his passage. About twenty feet back towards the crates, a man in a black shirt and blue jeans slowly pushed himself off the ground with a pained groan.

*Where the heck did he come from?*

Charlie looked back towards the crates, and at the top was a second man, partly covered by crates to his back and left. The other crates had been knocked away by the shock wave.

"Dammit!", the second man, whose dark skin was lighter than his dark blue shirt and faded blue jeans.

He saw Skid looking at him. He paled, then reached behind him with both hands. Skid didn't wait, and *accelerated* again. The shock wave picked up the first man and knocked him into the crates. The second man was hit by the first, and flew off at an angle as Skid put on the brakes, sending splinters and chunks of wood flying past him as he came to a stop. He trotted back quickly to the where the second man had been.

Finding the crates shifted, he trotted around to the other side of the huge pallets, looking for the man. He found him dazedly trying to push himself up off the ground. The first man lay prone at the front of the pallets, laying sideways, his face upturned, in a partly crushed wooden crate.

Skid ignored him and trotted over to the dark-skinned man, who groggily tried to take a swing at him and then fell face first on the wooden surface of the pier. Quickly flipping the man over, Skid took his belt off, then looped the belt over the man's hands and tied the end of the belt to one his legs, keeping his back arched so he couldn't loosen the belt and wiggle free. Once Skid was confident the crook wouldn't escape easily, he went to check on the first guy.

Skid found him still passed out, his face and clothes scratched and torn by flying wood splinters. Charlie swallowed, his throat dry with the realization of how dangerous his power really was.

*I got to find a better way. If I'd been moving faster, they might have been killed.*

Skid gingerly checked the fallen man for any visible broken bones and, seeing none, sped off the dock to look for Ms. Menendez and report what he'd found.

It took him a couple minutes to search the docks until he found her on the second pier south of the one where he'd encountered the two men.

"Hey! Follow me! I caught 'em!"

He waved his hands under the large lamp at the edge of the pier. The guard did a slow run to the car. She grabbed the open driver's door to help herself into the car, and then started it. Skid watched the lights flip on and ran in front of the car to direct her to the scene.

When they got there, Skid saw the man he'd tied up just starting to put his belt back around his pants. His eyes got wide as he heard the car, then he turned to run, only to trip over a foot that Skid had stuck in front of him. The man stumbled, and Skid deliberately body-blocked him into the crates.

"Freeze! I mean it! You don't move! Don't Move!"

Ms. Menendez was out of the car, a pistol drawn in one hand as she keyed her shoulder comm with the other.

"I got two men, broken crates. Seven-one. I repeat Seven One."

\*     \*     \*

The dark-skinned man groaned as he rolled over, and spread his arms and legs wide on the wooden pier as the Skid and Menendez waited for backup. It arrived at the pier in five minutes, along with a police cruiser.

The two men were handed over to the police while both Skid and the security guard's statements were recorded.

"How'd you find them?", the officer asked Skid.

"Uh," Skid hesitated. "I saw the crates out of alignment. When I went down the pier, I saw they were twisted. It looked like they'd been looking for something."

The officer looked at the heavy gouges in the pier, down towards the end, then back up near the front of the row of pallets.

"Any idea how that happened? Did the two suspects cause this?"

"Um, I never saw it happen. It looks like a big something was drug along. I don't think they could have done that."

The officer wrote down Skid's statement in his notebook. He looked at Skid, then down at his feet. The combat boots he wore were abraded down to almost nothing: the soles thin, the heels worn flat.

The officer raised his gaze slowly, then arched an eyebrow. "You're certain you didn't notice anything that might have caused this?"

Skid gulped.

*If I say yes, then I'm gonna get in trouble again. But if I say no, I'm lying to the man. I don't know what to do!*

"That came from one of the forklifts today," Ms. Menendez said. "Some dumbass tried to lift more than the fork could handle, and lost control of it."

The officer stared hard at the woman, who returned his gaze with her own, challenging him.

The officer straightened up, his eyes narrowing. "If you say so, ma'am." He started to put the notebook in his shirt pocket.

"Uh, sir, umm," Skid fumbled, sounding exactly like his seventeen years of age. "I uh, did that. I ran too fast and tried to stop too fast. That's what happened."

He looked down, face reddening in embarrassment, then looked up at the officer.

"I overran where I wanted to stop, and when I turned around, there they were one guy on the crates, the other on the ground."

The officer, jotted notes into his book. "I'm glad you came clean. I can put this down as collateral damage pursuant to capture."

Skid blinked at the officer, as did Menendez.

"Say what?" Charlie and Menendez said incredulously.

"It means it happened during the arrest, so the felons will be charged with the damage, not the person seeking to legally arrest them."

The officer smiled faintly, then stuck his notebook back into his pocket.

"Good work you two. Makes my job easier. But stay out of the habit. Getting involved is all well and good, but this could have gone down a lot different.

*Geez, I'm a hero, after all. Cut me a break.*

"Yes, sir," was what Skid said politely.

The other officers had finished putting the two men in the police cruiser. The two cars drove off, leaving the dock feeling much more subdued and quiet — or so it seemed to Skid.

"So, now that you got lucky, and caught 'em, what are you going to do?"

Skid looked at Menendez for a moment before answering.

"Go looking for trouble, I guess. Kinda what I'm supposed to do, you know?"

Menendez smiled. "Yeah, that suit makes it hard not to." She turned back to her car. "See you around, kid."

"It's Skid."

"Yeah, Skid."

She waved her hand at him and sat down in the car. A slight breeze brushed against her, and when she looked up, Skid had vanished.

Menendez chuckled, shaking her head.

"See you around, kid."

As Charlie sped towards the dock entrance, his heart felt ready to burst with excitement.

*I did it, I DID IT!*

# REDLEG

*This story came about from reading about an alligator attack in Florida, and from the music videos about the horrors and aftermath of combat. It also is kind of a curiosity about what happens when you begin dying. What goes through your mind? What experiences are there? Do you really see your life, or is that just some uniformed psychobabble that you're told just so that someone can sell their latest self-help book? This is another story I just started and it took off on its own ... to become what's written here.*

# 1

ARCHER "ARCHIE" GUNNISON WOKE to the strident buzzing of his watch. The cicada-like screech jolted him from sleep. His hands flailed about, seeking the offending noisemaker. His right hand finally caught up with his left and pressed the delay button, giving him a ten-minute window to wake up and turn the alarm off for the day.

Archie sat up in bed, letting the beige comforter droop into a pile on his lap. The dark blue curtains over the small bedroom window were closed, but the sharp, crisp air of autumn swirled through the open window, ruffling the cloth, letting peeks of gray morning flit across the bed. He yawned, then stretched his arms and good leg for a moment, enjoying the sensation of muscles waking up. He turned in place, dropping the right leg over the edge, then leaned down and picked up his prosthetic left one.

The leg was a marvel of engineering, fitted with self-adjusting spring tensioners. The covering for the prosthesis was something else again: bright, fire-engine red painted scales covered it — like some monstrous creature from the Red Lagoon. There was no way to ignore it — which was the reason Archie had it decorated. No one would mistake it — or him — for anyone else.

Archie gazed at the leg as he rubbed the stump of his left thigh. He was proud of his service as a Marine. Hoooah, boy, all the way. Proud of his buddies, and proud — and maybe a little envious — of the ones who made it home in one piece. He had left part of himself in a Hummer after an IED had blown it through three and a half revolutions before finally crunching back to earth. He didn't remember any of it.

What he did remember were the screams. He saw faces at night in his dreams. They would appear as people he knew — friends, family. Then they would change, becoming rotting flesh sloughing from ivory bone as they stared at him. Then they would scream and scream and scream until he would join them … and bolt awake sweating, screaming, looking for the enemy coming to do the same to him. The psychiatrists and psychologists worked with him. But, when he started seeing the faces from his dreams on the orderlies, he learned to sit quietly and nod. The less he drew attention to himself, the less the faces stared at him.

Six weeks of being quiet and nodding during therapy sessions fooled the doctors enough they turned him loose with a ticket home, and a prescription for Zoloft. He'd filled the prescription once, and then threw the rest of the pills down his toilet halfway through them. He hated the fuzzed-out feeling they gave him that made it so hard to think. He moved out of his parents' house, got a small apartment across town, then disappeared when the landlord demanded the three-months back rent he owed.

Then it was constant moving from one flophouse to the next. Or camping in the open, which he'd done plenty of back in-country. The flashbacks and screams haunted him, and he spent many sleepless nights trying to escape the screams and feeling of hopelessness that threatened to slowly swallow him whole.

The red-hot phantom pains were another matter. There was no telling when they'd strike. They seemed to happen mostly when he tried to dodge an obstacle without thinking. His leg would seize up, and he would drop screaming to the ground. After one too many vicious spills, he'd learned to think about the prosthesis before trying to do anything sudden, but the pain still occasionally caught him unawares.

He finished pulling the leg on, strapped it in place, then bent over again to pull the blue jeans from the floor. He slid them over his prosthesis first, then over his real leg.

He pulled on a rumpled green t-shirt next. The cartoon on its front was a coffin with a raised back, with two large tires on the rear and two small ones up front. The cab was black, except for two yellow eyes and a toothy smile from inside the cab. A cigar clamped between the teeth; the words "Coughin' Coffin" spelled out in smoke behind it. Standing up, he clumped awkwardly to the small storage drawers that served as his dresser.

Next to them stood his ankle-high black Converse sneakers. Made of canvas, they fit a little better around the fake foot, with just enough cushion to make walking feel semi-natural. Archie laced up the sneakers, grabbed the belt off the top of the left stack of drawers, then slid it through the loops on his jeans. He finished up by picking up the pack of cigarillos off the top of the right chest of drawers and slid one brown tube out. Grabbing his lighter off the right chest of drawers, he lit the cigarillo. The first smoky inhale centered him, and got him ready to face the day.

He slid the pack in his back pocket, the lighter in the front left, then he plucked his wallet off the drawer, shoving it into the left rear pocket. Another long inhale and exhale soothed the nicotine jitters, and he was ready for breakfast.

Archie clumped into the cramped kitchen, opened the dingy white cupboards over the sink, pulling out a box of strawberry toaster strudels. He grabbed the one remaining pouch, ripped it open, and dropped the pair of toaster strudels in the toaster. He caught them when they popped up, tossing them from hand to hand until they cooled enough to eat. He ate hurriedly, then grabbed his keys, hat, and cane before walking out the door. He locked it, then carefully trundled down the steps to the security door, and then out onto the sidewalk bounding Bleeker street.

The crisp taste of autumn rippled in the air like heat from the sidewalk. It penetrated the bitter exhaust fumes and damp, musty smog of the city. It spoke of the wild, open meadows, and dense old-growth trees that blotted out the sun even on a cloudless day. Downtown Baton Rouge was hardly ever this pleasant.

Most days were sweaty, muggy, and full of mosquitoes. Their constant whine of them near his ears had him waving his hands from his first moment out the door to his last moment in line to get a bowl of soup or stew at the local homeless kitchen. He often stayed after hours to help clean up, just to avoid those ravenous bloodsuckers before heading back to his small rathole apartment.

Archie's days melted together like overheated plastic. All the stimuli were depressingly — and comfortingly — unchanging.

He could set a watch to them. This sense of familiarity gave him comfort in his meaningless life. He could stumble through the day, without surprises, without changes so upsetting to his sense of stability.

There is a comfort not having hope. It's not ever going to get better, and won't ever change. Hope makes a person believe in the future, in a world actually caring about what happened to people. Archie didn't want hope.

He grimaced as he took his first shot of cheap gin. *Just to wake up,* he told himself — not very convincingly. The gin was his way of hiding from the world — and Archie very much wanted to hide. He wanted to hide from his memories, from the nightmares, and from the "concerned citizens" attempting to make his life better by telling the things he should do for himself.

Archie often thought of asking them why in God's name did they think he could do those things? If he was capable, he wouldn't be in this absolute craphole now, would he? Instead of screaming, he would duck his head, nod at the right moments, and then move on as soon as the person wound down. No use sticking around to hear everything again.

Archie ran a hand across the stubble on his face, grumbling yet again about having to see his haunted eyes in the mirror. Trudging the ten steps to the bathroom, with its toilet and leaky stand-in-the-corner shower, he didn't look up, not wanting to acknowledge his own reflection.

Reaching over to pick up the razor, he stopped. He lowered his hand and, in a fit of courage, raised his head. His reflection stared accusingly back at him, its sunken eyes bruised all the way around from lack of sleep.

The more he stared, the more angry and despairing he became. His rage beat stridently against his brain until the pain of it all closed his eyes and forced his arms around his body, trying to stem the self-recrimination. He had lived; his buddies hadn't. He lost a leg; they'd lost their lives. How in all creation was that fair?!

In a fit of blind, screaming despair, Archie threw himself into a frenzy of activity, pulled his one remaining boot on, slapped the locks on the prosthesis shut, and stumbled out the door, leaving his apartment unlocked. He stomped down the steps, hand jammed into his pocket, where the Beretta 9mm pistol sat, lethal and crying to be used. He planned on answering those cries — the ones in his head he couldn't stand any more. The eyes of his squad, the one he had been responsible for ... and failed. It was time to make the voices go away.

He turned east on Granville Street and began walking, head down, hurrying away from the emptiness he'd tried to live with. Granville arced to the northeast, and eventually crossed a rail line. This was what Archie had been looking for since he'd woken up. He had a purpose; he had a plan. He was on the way to execute the plan, follow through, where so many things he'd started never had.

He turned onto the rails: two shiny silver ribbons on top of blackish brown wood. The track went east, then angled slightly north of east, cutting a straight line through the dense vegetation and over the soft earth. It was easy to walk, and he did it, his mind focused on silencing the yammering in his brain, of getting the guilt of living off of him.

It was hours before he slowed and took a look about him. He'd gone close on to evening. The sun was a swollen yellow-orange tick just above the trees when he finally stopped walking. He wondered if his place had been stripped yet. Archie shrugged. It didn't matter anymore. It was a part of his life — just like the rest he was going to get rid of.

The crickets, frogs, and alligators offered their voices to the fast-coming night. It was nothing like Afghanistan. There, jackals might yip or yodel at night, but mostly it was the unceasing wind which ran icy fingers into his clothing, and had him burrowing into his cot when he wasn't part of a patrol.

His unit had gone through jungle training in Mississippi, and then got shipped to the high, cold desert. "God really had a sense of humor," one buddy had said, just before he took a round through his heart, and died, his blood pumping three feet in the air for a good two seconds before the combat medic slapped a huge bandage over the wound in a futile attempt to staunch it.

The medic had drunk himself off his feet that evening, puking and nearly drowning in his own vomit. Archie shuddered and screamed at the visions tearing at his sanity. He pulled the pistol from its hiding place in his pocket, and staggered forward, looking for...what, he wasn't sure. He'd planned on shooting himself after finding the perfect spot — a place where he'd fall in the water and disappear. But, as Archie learned in the Marines: no plan survives first contact.

# 2

ARCHIE TROMPED THROUGH THE FETID GREEN, now grey-green in the deepening dusk, towards open water. He tread carefully, old Afghan instincts clicking into place as he walked on the marshy ground. He didn't want to drown before he found where he wanted to be — which he found almost hilariously ironic, since his plan was to kill himself and not be found — and the area he now found himself in was as close to perfect as one could find. The mosquitoes and flies buzzed around him constantly. Normally, their attacks would have him trying to cover up by shrugging his coat over his head, but today he didn't mind their unrelenting thirst for his blood. He was beyond their petty hunger.

He crested a small mound to get a better look at the surrounding terrain. His boots *thonk*ed against a hard surface like rock, which startled him. In amongst the cypress, mounds made from vegetation clumped about the knobs rising above the water or were fallen trees. Rock was unusual. He shifted the vegetation with the toe of his boot. Under his foot, two stones fitted together so precisely, the line between them was only visible by the thin growth of moss that grew along the narrow space between them. Puzzled by this oddity, Archie straightened up, and focused on the surrounding terrain.

What he saw shocked him. Here and there in the boggy ground in front of him sat overgrown remains of buildings. To his left ran a long, low, irregular wall that undulated like a serpent. It rose out of the muck, then disappeared back into it again. Archie eyeballed it to be forty to fifty yards long — possibly more. Here and there, small portions of the wall dotted the landscape. Everything was so overgrown, Archie thought at first he was imagining all of it.

He pulled the grass away from the ground around his feet, exposing the edge of a circle. Curiosity welled up inside him, pushing away his thoughts of self-destruction. This was something he'd never seen before. He wanted to see what it was. Archie threw himself into kicking the plant life off the underlying rock and, eventually, the entire structure was exposed for the first time in untold years.

The circle itself was a ring of white stone inlaid the dull dark gray of another. A second ring of a shiny rose-pink rock nested a hand's span inside the white. Mud and detritus filled small carvings in both of the rings, making it look to Archie's eye like a magic circle from the fantasy movies he had loved so much before Afghanistan changed his life.

He stepped back with his artificial leg, then arched his back and shifted his weight forward, forcing the limb to bend into a kneeling position; his good leg bent at ninety degrees. Archie peered carefully past his knees to look at the stone. Absently waving mosquitoes away from his face, he recognized the white rock as quartz. The way the pink rock glistened made him think it was the same stone, though he'd never seen pink quartz before. He looked at the carved symbols, trying to puzzle them out.

His curiosity was torn away by a rumbling, grunting hiss that bubbled up right next to him, freezing Archie's blood in his veins. Once you hear that kind of sound, you remember it for life. He looked around frantically, trying to spot the angry 'gator. As he looked down, the hummock he was on came into focus. A small round mound with a dip in the center. He'd seen them many times growing up. The small mound he'd stepped on to get atop the stone was an alligator nest. How he'd managed to reach the nest without the mother alligator noticing didn't occur to him at all.

As he tried to run, the angry mother seized his artificial leg in her jaws and shook her head. Archie slammed down onto the stone, his hands scrabbling to find a grip and escape death. His frenzied struggles pulled the angry six-foot creature partly onto the mound. The mother alligator switched tactics, and rolled. The sharp edges of the quartz ring sliced her skin. Blood trickled on the white rock. The straps of Archie's prosthetic limb snapped and pinged from the monstrous stress, tearing it away from his body. Skidding across the exposed rock as he desperately tried to find a handhold, Archie sliced his hand open on the pink quartz. A sudden flash of light and a thunderous blast of sound erupted around him.

Electricity arced through his body. His back arched painfully. All of his muscles locked, and threatened to tear his body apart. His last conscious thought was that it was just like in the movies.

# 3

A RCHIE BELLOWED, AND TRIED TO SIT UP. A hard strap across his chest stopped him. A horse whinnied at the sudden shift and the noise. The travois to which he was strapped swayed back and forth as the rider struggled to control its skittish mount. Archie tried to move his arms, but the straps held him down. He screamed in anger, frustration, and fear. The horse shied violently at his screams, causing the rider to curse in some kind of whistling gibberish

It took a few moments for them to control the animal as Archie continued to fight the straps holding him down; the horse kept trying to bolt from the unearthly noise. Another person, a man, appeared beside him, sticking a sharp blade under his throat ... like an Afghan fighter readying to carve clear through his throat and spine.

Archie stopped struggling immediately. His eyes grew wide; he felt the sharpness of the blade against his skin. All thoughts of dying by his own hand long forgotten.

He looked up at his threatening captor, and nearly blinked in surprise. That he didn't speak could be attributed to the blade held in intimate pressure against his throat. The man's face was tanned, lined like one would expect with constant outdoor activity. His large almond eyes were almost too big for the lean face to contain them. His eyebrows were a thick, glossy brown, the kind of intense color one finds in a box of crayons. His eyes were a similarly intense yellow, like the color of ripened corn. His head was entirely bald, with no visible blemishes or scars.

Most startling to Archie were his ears. They resembled a teacup cut in half and glued to each side of his head. Offset slightly, they gave the man an odd, asymmetric look. The left "ear" rested slightly higher on the man's head, and also a little further back, than the other ear.

*Was it Halloween?*

The sun beat down, convincing Archie that it wasn't night — and this wasn't a practical joke. The man spoke a series of slow, liquid words, watching Archie's eyes closely. When Archie didn't answer, the man sighed, and stood upright. A rapid series of syllables received a reply from above him. The rider on the horse. The horse shifted uneasily, then the man stepped forward, out of Archie's view.

Archie tried to twist his head so he could see, but the skins holding the travois poles together would not let him see past his own shoulder. He heard the crunch of dry earth, then a few muffled thumps, like a person patting an animal. Then a measured tread and swish of dry grass as the rider walked back from the horse into view.

Like the man, her face was tanned and lined from constant drying in the wind. Her hair, too, was a deep, vivid brown, although lighter by a shade or two. Her eyes were also large and almond-shaped, but an intense dark brown, almost black. They seemed to hold Archie's gaze and threaten to swallow him. Her face was thin and long, though not grotesquely so. Both of her hands seemed odd to Archie. It took a moment before he realized they were malformed: only three fingers and thumb.

Archie looked away and down towards his legs. His right leg was there, flexing as he moved. The left one looked somehow more natural to him without the prosthetic. Then the image of what had happened came back in a rush.

The alligator, spinning on the edge of the circle, cutting itself on the white stone. The prosthetic breaking free of its harness and flying away somewhere. The thunderous blast of light, blinding and deafening, as he tried desperately to escape the jaws of the angry, protective mother. He wondered how he got here, how these people found him? With the dry wind and the blazing sun, how long had he been unconscious?

*Long enough, obviously, to strap him to a draggy thing behind a horse.*

Her hand grasped his, surprising him out of his musings. She looked at it, with its odd extra fourth finger where her hand had but three. His skin was much more pale than hers, bright pink now from the sunlight. He felt her hand as a cool touch on his sunburned skin. His face now made him aware of how dry and burned it was as well. Raising a hand to his face, feeling it warmed by the heat radiating from his cheeks — or so it seemed to Archie. She pulled his sleeve back, revealing the sallow pinkish-yellow skin that came from too much alcohol, and too little sunlight.

The man appeared next to the woman. The two of them looked at the large color difference between his hands and theirs. The man seemed to smile as he spoke in low, guttural trills and pops. The woman made the same face, which Archie thought might be a smile, though there was a mocking quality to it which set the small hairs on his neck prickling. The woman spoke again with those liquid-sounding trills. She finished speaking, and moved back to the horse, out of Archie's sight.

Archie spent the rest of the trip watching the man walking behind the travois, watching the sky, and watching the land — looking for anything alive besides the three of them. He didn't see anything. When the sky began to darken, its color shaded to an intense deep bluish-purple, and the two elves, as Archie decided to name them, helped him out of the straps. The male-elf steadied Archie as he hopped to the campfire.

Once there, Archie moved to the opposite side of the fire from the two elves, and then sat down.

He wanted space between them and him. He didn't think of escaping. How was a drunk with only one and a half legs going to outrun two healthy people? He couldn't outrun them, but he knew he could fight them. They were fast, but so was he. He didn't need both legs to fight. God knows having his other leg would help, but he felt confident of at least taking one of the two if it came down to that kind of thing. He hoped it wouldn't.

As he watched them cook something long and sinuous, he began to wonder where they'd found the wood. After looking about him, he guessed they must have carried it along with them, because there were no trees or brush for as far as he could see in the deepening twilight. The same for the water they used to cook the … whatever it was they threw in the metal pot hanging from a tripod over the fire.

He looked over towards the horse, and realized it wasn't one. It sounded like a horse, and it did have hooves, but its legs were bare, like those of a bird, from hoof to hip. What looked like broad, shaggy hairs covered its body, which Archie thought might be feathers.

Archie rose up smoothly on the one leg. The man-elf quickly came around the fire to assist him. Archie pointed at the horse-thing and started trying to hop towards it. The man helped him up, and supported Archie's stump-legged side as they walked over to the beast.

When they reached the animal, it shied violently away from them. While the man seemed to speak low liquid tones at the animal, it stayed at the far end of its tether, its oddly bowed front legs barely touching the ground as it seemed ready to slash with them.

Archie was close enough to confirm what he believed: the dark fur was indeed actually feathers. That he accepted it, he attributed to shock. He had to be dreaming all of this. There could be no other earth— ... otherworldly reason for all of this. He had to be asleep, and all this was one hugely detailed dream.

He must be dying; that's why the dream was so real. His mind was detached from the reality of his dying. The 'gator had got him, and now he was drowning as she had pulled him down to the bottom of the water, holding him there until he died. Then, when his body had stopped twitching, she'd shove his carcass into the mud to hold him down while he decomposed, all the better to rip pieces off when she got hungry guarding her eggs.

Archie looked the not-horse creature over. Along one of its sides a long strip of flesh had been carved from its body — almost exactly the same dimensions as the long thing the woman had thrown in the hanging cooking pot. It did not appear any worse for wear with the strip gone — at least as far as Archie could tell. Maybe it was in pain, and maybe it wasn't. He couldn't tell. If it was a dream, anything could be the case.

Archie thought it wasn't so bad to die, if this was what happened as the body quit working. He hobbled back to the fire with the man's help, and sat back down across the fire from them once more. He pondered the creature from where he sat; it had settled down again once they'd left its proximity. The man spoke a few liquid words again at the woman, then walked over to the creature, which reacted docilely to his approach, actually nuzzling his shoulder affectionately.

It was himself, Archie decided. He must smell terribly strange to the creature. *But why would it react in a dream? Because he wanted it to?* To test the theory, and convince himself it was a dream, Archie stood up, and began hopping over to the creature before the man could help him again.

The animal started pulling away from him as he approached. Archie concentrated and willed at the creature to calm itself. It fretted nervously as he closed the distance, but remained calm as Archie reached out to softly stroke its furry feathers, careful not to go against the grain. It actually leaned into his hand, as though it knew it had nothing to fear now. Its blunt, beak-like muzzle bumped him on the shoulder. The soft chirps behind him became fast and hushed. He chose to ignore them, and reached up to scratch along the openings on the side of its head where he thought its ears were.

Archie wasn't certain how long he stood next to the animal. He collapsed as his exhausted muscles suddenly cramped painfully. Dropping to the ground, he tried to straighten his right leg and stop the pain. The creature nuzzled his knee, as though understanding the source of his pain, but unable to do anything about it.

The man and woman quickly moved to him, straightened his leg and immobilized it, lessening the painful twitches of his muscles. They held it immobilized until the creature stopped fretting over him. Then, they released his leg slowly, and helped him stand upright.

They moved him back to his side of the fire, only this time they flanked him, and began a rapid-fire sing-song of guttural phrases, musical tones, sharp squawks, and many other sounds. Archie figured they were trying different languages in hopes he understood one of them. Unfortunately, none of them actually was remotely recognizable as a language to Archie. He tried English, then his smattering of Afghani, but, after no response, he gave up. They didn't seem to understand his speech any more than he understood theirs.

He tried to make them understand him like the horse-thing was able to, but they did not appear to notice his efforts or attempts to make mental contact. He finally accepted a blanket, and rolled up under it, while they lay theirs on the ground and rested on top of them, close together like lovers spooning in a bed.

*They probably were married,* Archie guessed. *Otherwise, why be together like this?*

Archie hunkered under the blanket, fighting to stay awake, to stay alive a bit longer, to see more of this strange dream he was experiencing. He felt cold, and wondered if his body was finally starting to die. The slight discomfort helped him focus his resolve to stay awake until the dream finished. But all the resolve is no defense against the body's needs, and Archie's eyes finally closed.

He fell into the waiting darkness, not expecting to wake up.

# 4

A GAINST HIS EXPECTATIONS, Archie awoke once more on the travois, strapped in place, as the man walked behind and the woman rode, guiding the creature towards their unknown destination. He wondered for a moment if they had one, then realized that, if he was dying, this could simply be a repeat of the last time: waking up on a litter and being dragged to who knows where as his body died — which seemed to be taking altogether too long. He hadn't expected to wake up, yet here he was, in the same dream all over again. They were traveling over the same terrain all over again ... or so he thought.

When the large bird dropped from the sky, landing just a few paces behind the man-elf, Archie was terrified that it would just swallow the unsuspecting man-elf up. Instead, it trilled at the man, who returned an apparent greeting in a similar whistling language. The man raised his arms, hands bent down at the wrist, and the bird did the same with its wings. They pressed the backs of the wrists together, then the man smiled and waved a hand in Archie's direction. They continued to slowly fall further behind the travois as they whistled, growled, and hooted at each other.

The woman chuckled — or so Archie guessed. She did not sound agitated. Neither did the horse-thing dragging him behind it. Archie scanned the countryside and the sky, searching to see anything beyond the featureless plain and empty air. He wondered if it was some kind of trick of his mind. If he didn't concentrate, nothing was visible. As the travois bumped along the ground, he tried to make things visible. He closed his eyes, then opened them again. Behind him, he now saw trees lining the road. Not many, and sparsely spaced apart, but real trees — or at least real dream trees.

Birds fluttered through the air — a few here, a few there — along with what looked like bat-like things that some of the larger birds seemed to hunt. The bat things were slower, but much more maneuverable. They turned on a proverbial dime in mid-air to avoid a lunge, their turns sharp enough to give nine cents in change.

Archie spotted more of the large bird creatures like the one that had greeted the man earlier. From the sounds ahead of their direction of travel, Archie thought it might be a group, perhaps the equivalent of a village. The cacophony of many voices swelled in volume as they continued forward.

The ground rose slowly and Archie could see some large trees to both sides. The trees appeared to have odd lumps growing from them as they continued approaching the noise. Now it came more from above him than at ground level. It took a few moments for him to realize that the lumps were huts.

Between the huts were living vines that looked braided into rope bridges.

It was more like what Archie had seen in the movies: elves living in the trees; bridges between residences; large flying birds dropping onto a perch by the house, to drop something off, or pick something up, with their huge, eagle-like beaks. One of the birds flew close overhead and Archie noted a difference between the eagles at home. Here, the bottom beak curved up rather than down, and looked like a scissor opening and closing. He shuddered at the thought of those jaws around his leg ... and his left knee suddenly burned like it had been dipped in molten rock. Archie clenched his teeth to keep from screaming, but the horse-thing sensed his distress and stopped, trilling urgently.

The woman dropped off her mount. Archie heard her feet smack the compacted earth, then a quick pattering She was next to him in a flash, looking for the cause of his distress. Her gaze focused on his half-leg, deducing somehow it was the cause of his pain. Archie thought it might be because he was dying, after all.

She rolled her left hand over her right, and then the right over the left, as if gathering something to her or pulling a fishing line in by hand. She hooted a regular series of notes. As she did, Archie thought he saw her hands begin to glow. As she continued working, he saw something start to form around his leg, and thicken around her hands. Instinctively, he realized what it was: a wispy blackish-red essence of pain, despair, and illness all in one miasma. It spun around her moving hands like yarn being gathered.

A popping sensation made Archie jump, then a sharp and painful tearing. He groaned aloud, and then the pain was gone with a proverbial snap of the fingers.

He lay there stunned. He hadn't been without pain since Afghanistan, after the bomb caught him. His body had been under such stress, it didn't know what to do now that the constant ache was gone. The lack of pain was like pain. His body, unfamiliar with the sensation, kept the remainder of his leg twitching constantly, as it had done to try an alleviate the constant phantom pain of his lost limb.

The woman suddenly groaned in agony, falling over as the miasma wrapped itself around her hands, extending up her arms to her shoulders. She writhed on the ground as the others who'd come to watch drew back from her. Archie was still strapped down, unable to move, but that didn't stop him from fighting the straps. He struggled to get free and help the woman. Then, she squawked painfully, pushed herself slowly off the ground, and stood upright.

She staggered back over to Archie, who watched her every step with trepidation. There was a purpose to her approach, which made him very uneasy. If she had been human, he'd call what he saw in her as hate. She hated him. More, she hated what she'd pulled from him.

*It must be part of the dying,* Archie reasoned. *My body's gone so far that it was shutting down, so the pain had gone away.* He wondered when it would be that he would close his eyes and forget everything.

She stood next to him now, then grimly kneeled next to the stump of his left leg. Her hands shot out, clamping painfully onto the stump's end. Archie sucked in a sharp breath as *something* flowed down her arms and into him.

His nerves came alive with pain so sharp it felt like he was burning alive. Strapped down, all he could do was scream and thrash in agony. He drew breath to scream again.

Then the pain stopped as if it had never existed. Archie gasped in shock. The sudden lack of pain left him disoriented. With the constant irritation of the phantom pain gone, he could feel everything once more, including the stump of his leg, but the phantom pain was gone.

He lifted his leg, studying it curiously. He thought he saw a faint glow, but it didn't go past the edge of the amputation. There was nothing: no tingling, no sensation of anything beyond the end of the stump.

The woman, however, gritted her teeth in obvious discomfort. Her movements were off-balance, just like she was learning to use a prosthetic. Archie had seen the same awkward movements when he was in rehab. Her stumbling shamble turned into a fall after two paces. The male elf, instead of helping her, took cautious steps away from the fallen woman. Archie thought he was waiting for her to ask for help ... or was reluctant to get close.

She pushed herself upright, and hobbled painfully towards her partner on the road. The male quickly stepped back again as she approached him, but remained close enough to control the still-skittish beast. The female-elf grabbed the solid loop at the front of the saddle, and pulled herself into the seat. The saddle had no stirrups, so her feet dangled on either side of the animal's body.

The creature calmed once the female was aboard it. Archie wondered if it was because of the familiar weight. The male stood next to the horse-thing and handed the female the loop of leather that ran around the creature's beak like a muzzle on a dog. Its large hooves were bad enough, but Archie suspected its beak was just as bad — or worse — at inflicting injuries.

Once the woman was settled, the man made sure Archie was strapped securely in the travois, then returned to the side of the woman, who clicked her tongue. Horse-thing, man, and woman all set out towards the sunset, with Archie once more being dragged behind on the travois.

Their travels were much like the last time, only now Archie constantly saw trees, birds, and those other things that looked like bats. It made him think it was all borrowed time — the kind of time you're never sure was yours to begin with, and never sure when it was going to end. Every night, he expected to never wake up, and each morning he did. Was he in a coma in a hospital? He believed he was dying, and all this day and night, travel and camping, had him half believing this was what the brain did to keep from going completely bugnuts crazy.

He was helpless still. They would unstrap him at night and, while they still attempted to communicate, there appeared to be no way either he or they could find a way to be understood.

In frustration one evening, he hobbled from his spot on the opposite side of the fire toward the other two. He dropped into a sitting position, grabbed a rock, then slapped it down in a bare spot, and scrawled a number "1" by it.

Both of them watched intently, but didn't interrupt. Archie snagged two more rocks, and dropped them under the first. He wrote "2" next to these, then did the same with three rocks. The last one burned his hand slightly when he pulled it away from the edge of the fire. Archie pointed at each number, and held up the corresponding fingers. After three slow indications with both rocks and fingers, he pointed at the male, then at the rocks.

To his surprise, the man arranged the rocks *exactly* as Archie had first set them out: everything from rocks to any debris — including burning himself lightly as he arranged the last rock in the "3".

Archie was ready to tear his hair out. They didn't see what he did as numbers, but as a picture. He punched the ground in frustration.

*A picture. How was he supposed to explain that each one was a separate value, rather than a tapestry?*

Archie did reluctantly give credit where it was due. How many humans could exactly reproduce what they saw down to the smallest detail? It galled him beyond reason, but also fascinated him. He tried constructing a picture of himself riding the horse-thing, with the male in the travois and the female guiding it. The two of them looked hard at the picture, then the male erased the travois, and put himself guiding the mount, and the woman next to him. Archie stared, then went back to his former spot by the fire.

# 5

THE NEXT MORNING, the male helped Archie to the side of the mount, then made an emphatic-sounding *"wheet"* as he pointed at the saddle. Archie grabbed the hard loop, which he determined might be made of leather covering wood. Bending his one remaining knee, Archie jumped as best he could, pulling on the ring at the same time.

He sprawled across the saddle, belly down. It took only a moment for him to spin face forward and straddle the beast with his thighs. One leg hung down; the amputated one ended in line with the bottom of the beast's chest. His body kept leaning to the right because of the extra weight of the whole leg. The two elf-people rasped, *wheet*ed, and clacked their jaws as they apparently argued about Archie being on the mount. While they continued to pay attention to each other, Archie tapped the animal's flanks gently like he'd seen the rider do before, and the creature lurched into motion.

Archie nearly fell off at the first jolt. He grabbed the ring and steadied himself, earning a look back by the beast and the sudden screeching of both beings behind him. The male ran up next to the saddle ring and grabbed at it, while simultaneously reaching for the loop of leather Archie had forgotten to grab from around the beast's neck.

He held it still until the woman had painfully loaded all the gear on the travois, including the six rocks he'd used to try and show them counting. Once everything was secured, the woman grasped the leather muzzle and wobbled alongside the mount as the man once again walked behind the travois. Archie wondered if it was to watch him or the supplies. Ultimately, it didn't matter. He was at Archie's back and hadn't done anything to make Archie's survival instinct kick in.

He looked back again at the man, trying to decide what it was he should be doing. Since the mother alligator had torn off his prosthetic, things had been chaotic: with being strapped on a platform, some kind of ritual, people who thought in pictures, and, as yet, he'd no idea what they were doing, or where they were going, or for what reason. That he had no clue at all was maddening.

Archie rode for most of the day. During the ride, he had to constantly pull himself back on center as his heavier right leg kept dragging him off-balance in the slippery saddle. He'd managed to stay upright until their small troupe stopped for the evening.

Bedrolls were laid out, and Archie studied the night sky that blazed forth with stars that made his own view back in Baton Rouge feel sterile. It was like the lights of the city sucked all the glory of the night sky away, leaving a dull, empty curtain with only a very few dots of light looking more like holes eaten in dark cloth by moths. Here, light coursed through the night — alive, with flickering lights like thousands of small fireflies. The amazing view of the stars caused him to think back to his childhood, watching the stars at night, listening to the crickets and frogs chorusing in the still summer air.

Then his mind went to Afghanistan, and how the night always held death in its dark arms; how those arms would open and rain terror down on their position. The anticipation of another attack like then caused him to hyperventilate as his heart began to speed up. He rolled onto his side, gasping for air as his heart raced a thousand beats a minute. The panic attack gripped him tight. The overwhelming fear swallowed his rational self and he launched himself off the ground, balancing on his one leg, frantically looking around for the threat, shouting fear-crazed rage into the air. His barking screams threw the entire camp and surrounding area into chaos.

The horse-thing tore madly at its muzzle, trying to free itself, its eyes rolling in terror. Both of the elves bolted upright, shoulders rolled forward, their arms open and angled downwards. They looked like birds mantling to threaten away a predator.

Archie saw only threats, and knew, with one leg gone, he was hurt bad. He had to be bleeding out. But, by god, he was *not* going to die without taking them with him. His buddies were out there somewhere in the dark; he had to keep these killers away from them. He started to bring his M4 up to aim, then realized he didn't have it in his hands. He looked down. He wasn't in uniform. There was no blood, no pain. He couldn't figure out what was going on.

Something blurred in front of his eyes. Something hard rammed into his stomach, knocking him sprawling. Screaming in fear and rage, his hands going to the sides of the Afghani's face. He bunched his muscles and brought his one knee up, landing a solid blow to the body on top of him. Immediately shifting his grip, he used one hand to push desperately against his attacker's chin, the other at the back of the head to tear it forward.

His arm was seized and pinned. He snarled and turned to look at his attacker, only to find a woman's face near his own. The surprise of her tearing his arm loose and holding it froze him for a critical second. She took full advantage of the momentary confusion, battering him with her fists. The first blow to his head dazed him; the following flurry smashed him into unconsciousness. His thoughts, as the light faded away, were that maybe now he had finally died.

# 6

ARCHIE WOKE UP in a frustratingly familiar situation. He was bound and back on the travois. The woman was likely riding the mount since the man walked next to Archie. Archie watched him glance down in his direction, then took a step to the side, taking him just out of arm's reach. His demeanor had changed drastically. Where the man had been cautious but curious before, now he was hard-eyed and suspicious. Archie felt the man's attention lock on him with every slight movement he made.

In the evening, he remained trussed to the travois. The woman left the travois connected to the beast, and now brought a bowl of food for Archie. She placed the bowl down on the ground, then worked the straps holding his arms. She stepped back three paces, and then crouched like a bird watching a potential predator.

Archie reached down to carefully pick the bowl up. It held stew with some kind of meat. Archie guessed it was another strip from the mount. He wondered again if the animal felt pain from the meat they harvested from it. It didn't seem to be hurting the last time, and ... Archie's stomach chose to protest that he'd not eaten in quite a while, and would he please do so, now?

The flavor of the stew was exotic, and smelled like a hot pepper. He was surprised by its intense flavor with no spicy heat. Archie upended the bowl, chewing and swallowing hungrily. After he'd licked the bowl clean, during which the woman had stared intently at him, he set the bowl down and turned his head away from the woman and her intense gaze.

Moments later, he heard the scuff of her shoes on the dry ground. He kept his head turned away, unwilling to face her after his maniacal actions earlier, afraid the elves were upset. Archie knew it was irrational. They'd given him food, and hadn't just kicked him to the curb like so many others had since he'd gotten home. The shame of his fear-crazed attack on his companions made him squeeze his eyes shut, trying to hold in the pain of screwing his life up further.

It was asinine. He knew it was something he couldn't control. But all the talking with psychiatrists, the brain-deadening pills, and his own desire to be away from people, didn't stop the urge to isolate himself. It happened. He couldn't stop himself any more than he could will his friends back from the grave.

He took a shaky breath when he didn't hear the footsteps anymore. Archie guessed that the elf-woman had taken the bowl and walked back to the campfire while he was excoriating himself. He stared at the thick grey blue mat of moss-like vegetation, running his hand over it as he tried to soften the shame he in which he had wrapped himself. He was so focused on his own misery, he didn't notice two hands descend, then press against his cheeks.

Stifling a yell as his head was forced to turn to the left, he started to pull away, but the gentle hands held him firmly. She turned his head until he stared directly into her eyes mere inches away from his own. Her hands moved slowly along his face and neck, pausing here or there on a bony area, then shifted to the top of his head.

Here, they paused, and seemed to grow warmer. He stayed still and focused on her touch. She remained in front of him, hands on his head for a minute or so longer, then withdrew them. She made what sounded like a *wheet* of frustration as she walked back to the man. The two rasped and warbled for a good while as Archie looked around. He concentrated on seeing and, slowly, to his surprise, things faded into view, as if he'd willed them into being.

He remembered doing this earlier, and wondered if it was because he was in a coma that the dream was still ongoing. He listened to the two talk — or argue, or whatever they were doing. Archie knew he couldn't understand them, except they used pictures to talk. The thought suddenly gave him an idea.

With his hands free, it was easy to undo the other straps, which was maybe what the woman had intended. He thought about how to use what he knew. He looked at the supplies on the ground next to the horse-thing. In the packs were the stones. He pulled them out, dropping them on the ground next to the packs.

His neck hairs prickled as someone's gaze focused on him. The sensation so alarmed him that he dropped onto the stump of his left leg, his right extended in a ground defense stance. He spun to his left, searching for the threat, and saw the two staring at him with the searing intensity of hot sunlight on cold skin. Archie returned the stare for a moment, then lowered his gaze and turned to the packs. Rummaging through their contents, he finally found a long piece of a light metal which had a long, sharp edge.

He walked away from the camp. Once he'd gotten some twenty wobbling paces past the tethered horse-thing, he lowered down onto his left stump and began cutting the moss away from the dry ground. He cleared a long strip, then started using the metal to cut scratches in the ground.

It was clumsy, but he kept focused on his work until he finished a series of very crude pictures. It showed a stick man with one long and one short leg. In the next drawing, the man with the short leg received a lower leg from another stick person. The next picture showed the stick man losing the prosthetic leg to a low-slung four-legged monster. Then there was just the stick man with half a left leg. The final panels showed the stick man getting a peg leg to use, and then the stick man standing on the peg leg.

As Archie finished, the sun peeked over the horizon. He'd worked through the night to make the scene. Archie gazed at the sleeping pair, and gritted his teeth in frustration.

There was no reason for it. Archie was sick of it all. He couldn't talk, couldn't help, couldn't flat communicate with anything. He hadn't felt alone like this, ever.

He hadn't thought of it, but not being able to communicate was the worst thing he'd encountered since this all started. It ate at him. He was alone by choice when he was in the real world. Here, when he wanted to socialize the most, it seemed impossible.

Archie hopped back towards his place on the opposite side of the fire. It was so stupid. He couldn't even ask for a stick to help him walk. His leg gave out the last ten yards. He'd worked so obsessively through the night that it had become severely overworked. Now it cramped, causing him to collapse to the ground in pain and frustration.

Archie pounded the ground in rage, so caught up in failure that he didn't notice the man and woman peering at the pictures. He gritted his teeth and crawled slowly the rest of the way back to his spot, the muscles in good leg screaming at him the entire way. Once he returned to his customary spot, he shifted into a sitting position and began to knead the overworked muscles. It took a good half hour of massaging for the cramp to relax enough so he could straighten the leg out. The man and woman had gone back to the mount, and seemed to be communicating in low and intense *wheets* and chirps. It was totally unlike their normal interaction, and Archie was drawn to watch.

He wondered if he would ever learn to communicate with them. They'd fed him, cared for him, and carried him, it seemed, everywhere. Archie knew this had to be a dream, and he had to be either in a coma, or dying. It was the only reason he could think of which fit the logic of it all.

Now, instead of wanting to communicate, he decided to stop trying and just give up. He had finally had enough. He was ready to die. He curled up in the thin blanket, and lay there through the morning, despite the noise he could hear from where the beast was tethered.

He heard the clatter of things being packed, listened to the hoots of soft protest from the horse-thing as it was loaded with the travois and the equipment. The blanket was ripped off him, catching Archie by surprise. Every other time he'd woken late, they'd patiently waited for him to perform his morning toilet before he hopped onto the bed to be strapped down again.

Something had changed. He never had them be so abrupt. They seemed impatient to be moving.

*Why had their routine changed?*

Archie liked routines. Routines made it easy to do those things you needed to do, and not have to think about it. Thinking made his memories wake up — things he didn't want to think about, or even remember. An alcoholic stupor was the only way to quiet them down once they started in on him. Which was another revelation.

In all the time he had been here, he hadn't craved a drink, or a smoke. In fact, he hadn't had any dreams either. This made sense to Archie. After all, if he was dying, he'd had a drink this morning, and it wouldn't wear off until after lunch sometime. If he was in a coma, the DT's probably couldn't register. His mind was probably too deep into itself for anything to bother him.

*So why in all the world — or, all his imagination — were these dreams forcing him to move?*

The answer had to be survival. His mind must have decided to shut down, but his body fought to go on. Mind versus body. The female lifted Archie, using only one arm by wrapping it around his waist like a steel cable. She trotted over to the travois, then laid him on it gently, almost reverently, which confused Archie further.

*Why be so gentle now, when he finally made up his mind about something?*

This time, they traveled much faster. The man trotted alongside Archie, as the woman ran next to the mount, both of them covering ground with long loping strides. As they moved, the beast worked to match its gait to theirs. The frame on which Archie lay bounced and wobbled like a drunk after an all-night spree. After fifteen minutes of it, he thought he was going to be sick. After close to an hour of the grueling pace, he was.

He was able to lean to his left just enough he didn't throw up on himself or the travois. The man and woman ignored it and kept moving at the fast double-time. Archie had never seen people keep a pace like the one they did. They seemed tireless.

Archie knew even with two good legs, his youth, and all the military training, he'd still be gassed after a half hour. People just aren't made to run so far for so long. He wondered why his imagination would come up with something so nonsensical.

*He wanted to die, didn't he?*

*Maybe he did?*

Archie watched the greenish-gray waste flit along like scenery from a train window. Things would be slow in the distance, and almost a blur up close. Even running, the two of them kept up with whistles, gargles, hoots, and *wheets*. The faster they moved, the louder their calls were back and forth, with Archie wishing desperately he understood what they were saying.

The little group didn't stop for lunch, running through the normal rest break like it was something they always did. Their intensity seemed to rub off on him. Archie found himself wanting to go faster, to see what they were trying to reach.

He thought it must be an important place. Why else push so hard? Was it a city, or a fort? The idea of a fort out here seemed incongruous. There was nothing to hide anyone out here. Then he remembered Afghanistan. The tribesman seemed like they could hide under a twig on the ground. Ambushes were all too common, and often too hard to spot, before the Afghani rose up and began firing. He and his buddies hadn't been caught — mostly through sheer luck — but squads they knew had been, and most of those had lost people.

The memories made him wonder if this area was dangerous somehow, and this was why they ran so hard. Was the danger an animal, a hostile group, or something natural like a volcano? Archie had no clue. The only thing he knew was they seemed to run even harder once they got onto a large stretch of flat ground.

It was well after sundown when they finally slowed to let the horse-thing catch its breath. The animal's sides heaved with effort as it tried to pull in enough air to allow it to recover. The man and woman unloaded the beast, and set up camp just like any other night. The only evidence they had exerted themselves in any way was the slower pace in which everything was done.

Once the campfire was started, Archie was unbuckled and lifted gently from the travois by the female. She carried him using both arms, and deposited on the far side of the fire, as he preferred. Both the man and woman watched him closely with an intensity he'd not experienced since the first night he appeared in this place, which now seemed so long ago. He questioned himself yet again what had changed since the night he made the pictures.

He froze. It was the pictures! It had to be. It was the day he'd decided to die. He was so tired of being alone and not able to talk or communicate with anyone. He still ached for a way to understand them. More than anything, he wanted to know why those pictures had them so determined to get somewhere.

He wondered if they understood the pictures. All he wanted was a wooden prosthetic for his bad leg, then he could walk with them for a while. It was demeaning to be carried like a baby on a pack frame. His leg no longer ached like it had in the past. There was no phantom pain — no matter how stressed he got or how tired.

He gazed over at the man and woman, noticing that she seemed to have gotten over whatever had been making her act like she was drunk or in great pain. After finishing the cooking, she sat down, her legs straight. The man reached over and massaged her lower left leg. Archie wondered why. He remembered the red and black smoke, and how it seemed to emanate from his leg and move to the woman. He wondered if it had been some kind of dream, or a metaphor for the state he was really in — or if it was simply "white noise" as his body continued to shut down. It all made his head hurt. He lay down, expecting never to wake up.

The morning, however, saw him being lifted and set gently on the travois, and then strapped in. Then they were off once more at the same quick double-time pace as the day before. The group ate up the miles, always heading just south of where the sun rose in the morning.

Around an hour or so later, the ground began to shift from low, mostly flat, ground to more uphill and broken. He felt they must be approaching whatever destination his failing brain was creating as a way to stave off his final death. It had to be. All of this strange activity had to lead to something.

He was in the jaws of an angry mama alligator. Everything else was simply his brain refusing to get the idea his body was dead, and it would be too — very soon. The thought oddly comforted him, and he looked forward to seeing what his dying imagination would gift him with.

He wasn't disappointed.

# 7

CRESTING THE LAST TALL FOOTHILL brought him a view of a large bowl carved from the back side of the hill. It arced out and down in both directions, its edges dropping sharply to a flat area filled with vibrant yellow-green. Archie knew instinctively it was a marsh. The vivid color meant there must be copious amounts of water there.

He experienced a moment of panic as the two coaxed the horse-thing to the sharp, vertical cliff, then started along a barely-wide-enough ledge which meandered back and forth down the cliff face. He shut his eyes in fear, then stubbornly forced himself to watch and experience their descent.

This had to be the end. He had always had a fear of falling, and this must be something about fear being a part of him taking his final breath. He thought it had to be, after how long this dream had held him. It was finally time.

As he found out, "finally time" took a long time. The sense of hours passing as the group made their delicate descent to the base of the small mountain had Archie brimming with impatience.

The bright foliage he had seen from the top of the foothill became hummocks of grass that grew taller than he could reach if he were standing — at least nine feet in height. They had a swampy wet look to them, and the first splash of the horse-thing's hooves in water confirmed it. The water never got high enough to get him wet. The slow pace he was pulled through the marshes likely prevented that.

After they had traveled for about five minutes, the ground rose again. The travois stopped. Peering to his left, Archie could see dry ground for quite a ways. They had to be on a large patch of it. His two companions, as he had come to call them, walked back to the travois and unstrapped him. The male took his weight and helped Archie stand up. The female lurched suddenly, hooting in pain. The man stiffened, then stopped to watch as the woman clumsily stumbled forward towards something that looked somehow familiar to Archie.

The ground ahead was grayish, with a whitish circle within. A deeper almost-black circle lay inside the white circle. It looked identical to the place where he lay dying outside the dream. With a growing sense of equal parts anxiety and anticipation, Archie wondered if this was the last stop in this dream.

*Back to the 'gator and the circles?*

The wind whipped wildly around him and the others. Fingers of ice ran along his body wherever the wind could reach. He shivered and tightened his hand on the male's shoulder. The man whistled quietly as his body tried to hunch over and away from Archie, but he could not escape Archie's fierce grip.

They awkwardly stumbled forward, following the female as she continued towards the circle. As Archie watched the woman struggle to keep her balance, the wind whipped up sand and dirt from the ground into an opaque dust devil at the other side of the rock. The dust devil fell into itself as the wind seemed to pick up. It churned wildly as it shrunk down to man size, then faded, revealing a tall, human-looking being on the far edge of the circle.

Clad in bright teal-colored pants and a cloak, straps across his chest held two large knives against his hips. Thumbnail splotches of brown and white spotted his hair. He stood, arms relaxed at his sides, and stared silently at the small group.

The new male remained silent and unmoving as the female approached. She attempted to bow, or kneel — Archie wasn't sure which — but the attempt turned into a crumpling fall as she hooted in pain. The other being moved forward slowly towards her, then actually offered her a hand up. It was the first time Archie had seen anyone offer to help another in this place.

The situation was short-lived as the new male squawked in apparent surprise and pain when his hand was grasped by hers. He let go of her hand and stepped back, his hair frizzed out like a cat with its tail stuck in a wall socket.

He made a jagged, painful sound somewhere between a screech and a whistle. The air seemed to vibrate with the agony of the being's exclamation. The horrid tone made Archie's eardrums feel like they might explode during the brief moment the noise lasted. The answering heaviness from all around reminded Archie of the muggy air back in Baton Rouge just before a big thunderstorm.

The new male hooted a question at the female, who was trembling. What Archie thought might be sweat beaded out on her forehead and arms. Her body appeared stretched taut as an overtightened string. Only her will seemed to be keeping her upright as the male moved to Archie's side, and unstrapped him from the travois.

A flash of lightning in the distance was followed, by Archie's count, four seconds later by the faint grumble of thunder. Archie realized the section of the mountain they were on was at the same height as most of the surrounding peaks. and this one was still a quarter taller than those around it. He wondered if they were going to wait the storm out in the open, or if there was a cave nearby. He hoped for waiting in a cave.

The elf-male helped Archie up, acting as a walking support for Archie while he hobbled along the narrowing trail ever upward. The trail wound upwards for several hundred yards before it reached a flat area.

It turned out there was no cave. Instead, there was a number of beehive-like structures constructed from piled rocks which could double as shelter. Archie tried to guess which one they were going to put him in. To his surprise, and growing concern, they ignored the beehives. The Priest, Archie decided to call him, turned to his right and led them towards a small path that wound towards a split in the rock.

Once past the gap, the path pitched up sharply. Archie noticed steps carved into the rock. The Priest led the three of them up steps that switched back and forth ever higher along the cliff face.

The steps were wide enough for four men to walk shoulder to shoulder, with a platform about ten paces wide at the point where the steps changed direction. The Priest paused only long enough for Archie and the male helping him to catch up, then started briskly up the next set of steps.

Archie and the man helping him struggled to keep up with the female, who was laboring up the steps nearly as badly as Archie was. She favored her left leg, making exaggerated, careful movements up to the next riser, then almost hopping to keep weight off of it. *Tap-hop, tap-hop,* each two steps. Archie was doing nearly the same dance up the stairs, only he had another person to lean on, and his left stump didn't hurt at all.

The stone staircase wound back and forth, ever upward. The temperature fell steadily, the smell of ozone becoming more pronounced. Lightning flashed in the distance at what Archie thought was eye level, meaning they were going to be at the same height as the approaching storm, if that's what the bright flashes really were.

The ozone smell became a sharp acidic burning in his sinuses which made his eyes water. The clouds drifted over and around the group, reaching the edge of the small plateau, then parted like water being sliced by the bow of a ship.

*No,* Archie thought. *That wasn't right.*

It was more like something was at the tip, forcing the clouds to part. They went left, right, and over something, always staying clear of the narrow, flattened walkway that they were on. As the grey wall advanced over them, Archie compared it to being swallowed. The gray surrounded them, blotting out everything but the Priest, the walkway, the man, the woman, and himself.

As the Priest continued to lead them towards the edge, a faint reddish haze began to form. The Priest stopped just short of the edge. The woman hobbled next to him, and then sank bonelessly to the ground. Soft moans of what Archie recognized as pain came from her as the man helped him forward.

Light began arcing overhead, crashing to the ground outside the tunnel of gray, lighting everything in relief for a bare instant before darkening until the next bright strike. The reddish haze solidified when it reached the side of the Priest, coalescing into a tree with a red trunk and branches festooned with bright yellow leaves. It stood rooted at the very edge of the plateau, its bow splitting the mist.

As the Priest approached, he threw his hands out in front of him, spreading them wide. A section of rock rose from the solid-looking ground, then widened and lengthened to resemble a rectangle. The Priest lowered his arms. The top of the platform sunk in the middle, forming a bowl. As the Priest spread his arms out again, the bowl stretched and became vaguely man-shaped. Archie watched with uneasy interest as the rock reshaped itself — wet clay in the hands of a sculptor.

*Could this be a sacrifice?*

A scene flitted into his mind of his body lying in the depression as the Priest cut his heart out. He swallowed dryly at the vividness of the thought, and attempted to calm himself by reasoning they wouldn't just cart him all this way simply to kill him.

*It isn't killing,* the little voice in his head chirped at him. *It's a sacrifice.*

Of course they would, if it was important to them. They'd truss him up like a hog for slaughter. They'd be respectful to the strange arrival, like you, and offer a sense of camaraderie, like you, then lead him to a pedestal, like you, and cut your throat wide open. Of course, if you believe you're dead, it won't matter much, will it? It'll be all over, and this grand dream will blink out, because, well, death.

Archie felt fear — honest to '*ohmygodImgonnadie*' fear. He didn't struggle because, even in this dream, it felt surreal. Whatever was happening, personal or not, it was just a dream. He couldn't force himself to fight. He wanted to — Lord, he wanted to — but something kept him complacent and cooperative.

He remembered it from lectures, about how a person, knowing they were going to die, cooperated because it let them live just a little longer. Even as the fear of death held him tight, he wondered if this was part of this dream: the fear was the nightmare part, and his body had purposely gone limp to avoid hurting itself. He couldn't stop stumbling forward, and couldn't stop the terror from building inside him.

The male supporting him stumbled as Archie went limp with fear. He reached down and cradled Archie's lower leg and stump in one arm, like a man cradling a sleeping child. He walked over to the pedestal, and placed Archie into the man-shaped depression. He stepped back as the female moved awkwardly forward. She still looked like she was getting used to a prosthesis, Archie's terrified mind observed dispassionately.

She braced herself against the altar and slid her hands into the depression below the stump of his left leg. She looked back to the Priest and made a soft chirping, buzzing sound which seemed like a query. The Priest, his arms hanging down, raised them to the side, making him look like a cross. As he did, the depression in the rock molded itself to Archie. The portion where his lower left leg would lay was empty, except where the woman's hands rested in it. Pale and sweating, she hunched over, her upper body quivering with effort as she forced her hands to remain in place.

She turned her head to gaze intently at the Priest, who raised his hands overhead, palms flat together like in a yoga pose one of the volunteers at the Veterans Administration had shown Archie as a way to let go of stress. As the Priest's palms met, the woman screamed. Her throat sounded like the pain was being ripped out of her. A tremor started in her body, rolling up into her neck. Her head whipped around like a shaken bobble-head doll. Archie broke out in a cold sweat as the tremor shifted into her shoulders, went from her upper to lower arms, and then to her hands placed in the depression.

The pedestal vibrated. A vicious droning came from the rock and Archie felt suddenly paralyzed. His mind went into overdrive.

*Sacrifice! Sacrifice! Sacrifice! Sacrifice!*

Ihe word pounded on him like hammers. When the woman screamed again, he saw the limbs of the red tree lower towards him. The branches and leaves resembled grasping hands — or an open mouth filled with teeth. A thick red branch seemed to push the female away and, as she stumbled back, PAIN roared into him like an angry lion. The paralysis wouldn't even let him scream. He had to endure it all in helpless silence as the stump of his leg burned like being dipped in fire and held there.

The last sensations he experienced were hearing a cracking sound, the shouting of the Priest, and sudden blackness as pain surged through him. Every muscle locked rigid as the air in his lungs turned to ice.

He fell into the dark.

# 8

T HE WAILING OF SIRENS WOKE HIM. Archie groaned, trying to move, but found his arms and legs were strapped down. A man in a light blue uniform looked down at him. The whole room, which seemed small, wobbled back and forth, its equipment shifting as the room lurched suddenly to the right.

"Damn asshats! Can't you see us!? We got sirens and lights dammit! Outta the way!" came from somewhere past his head.

Archie looked back up at the man in the blue uniform, who gave him a smile and a thumbs up.

"You're going to be okay, buddy. Some folks heard ya scream when they saw the 'gator jump ya. Damnedest thing for lightning ta hit there."

He flashed a light in Archie's eyes, which normally would have him screaming from the resemblance to the IED flash when his team died. Now, however, he could hold himself together with no trouble.

He wondered why.

The EMT continued with his banter, working at putting Archie at ease. "One-twenty over seventy, seventy beats even. Equal dilation. Ninety-eight-point-four," he stated professionally to the person up front, and Archie heard the man relay the details.

The EMT turned back to Archie, looking him over for wounds or bruises. "Anyhow, folks heard ya screaming, an' hauled ya outta the water an' called us. You're fine, but darned if I know how. The folks said both you an' the 'gator were hit by the bolt." The EMT paused a moment. "Not a cloud in the sky, neither. Heh. First time I can say to anyone they were hit by a bolt from the blue."

It was such a literal statement to Archie that he chuckled, and the EMT laughed out loud.

"So Mister ... ahh ..." the EMT flipped open Archie's wallet, "... Gunnison, we have to take you into the hospital, since we rolled with you being unconscious and all. The docs oughta let you go after a quick check. You must be a lucky guy to survive an angry 'gator and lightning at the same time. Maybe you oughta get a lottery ticket."

The EMT looked down towards Archie's legs.

"You know, you're the first guy I've met who went old school with a peg leg. Most of 'em now go for the fancy prosthetics. For an old, red piece of wood, it's sure stuck on tight. I couldn't figure out how that darn thing stays on." He shrugged. "Ah, well. Not anything I need to worry about. Your leg's fine, so no reason to try and get it off." He checked his cellphone. "A minute out, you just lay back and we'll have you out of here in no time."

# … AND A CREATURE
# WAS STIRRING

*This story comes from personal experience. We picked up a ferret as a pet, and she proved to be an adept escape artist — and relentlessly curious about everything she came across. The Christmas tree was a perpetual target while it was up, and it was that first night that all the chaos written here came about. Rascal, and her partner in ferrety mayhem, Mischief, are gone now, but they left many, many precious memories that I will cherish.*

# … AND A CREATURE
# WAS STIRRING

Louis Grummle groaned as a sharp object poked him in the ribs. He grunted obligingly and rolled towards his side of the bed, giving Bev the space she wanted. The new spot was cold, and he curled his legs up to help stay warm. The sharp object (he was awake enough to recognize Bev's finger) poked him in the back this time, just above the short rib. His twitch reflex made him inhale sharply.

"I'm awake, I'm awake," he said with a resigned groan. Bev obviously had noticed something, otherwise she wouldn't have woke him up.

"Louis, you left the lights on downstairs," Bev said with an irritated sleepiness. "You know I can't sleep with lights on."

"Right, right," Louis mumbled. Rather than argue, which guaranteed he wouldn't get any sleep, he rolled away from Bev, swung his legs of the side of the bed, and sat up.

Louis, clad only in a white tee-shirt and black boxer shorts, shivered as goosebumps formed on his skin from the cold caress of the night air. He reached for his bathrobe and quickly put it on. The thick maroon terrycloth warded him against the chill, and the carpet kept the floor warm, despite the cold air.

*One thing we could agree on: we both liked the cold to sleep in. But it's a bitch to wake up to.*

They'd set the thermostat to let the house drop overnight to fifty-eight degrees, and then warming up by five in the morning to a balmy seventy — plenty warm to wake up comfortably to. It was a delicious feeling to be so warm at daybreak, shower, then wander downstairs to share a cup of coffee and a plate of eggs with toast in the small kitchen.

Finishing shrugging into the bathrobe, Louis pushed his feet into his year-old Cheshire Cat slippers (their daughter had gotten them for him last Christmas). With mauve and grey stripes, and wide white grin, their absurd and mischievous appearance always gave him something to smile about. It was, he reflected fondly, one of those presents that grew on you.

He straightened with a grunt, then walked to the door and opened it.

*Might was well get it done, though now that I'm up, a snack might be …*

It was then that the light downstairs went out. A cold chill raced up his back.

*Someone's in the house?! What do I do?! The phones are in the kitchen downstairs. We can't call for help!*

His legs suddenly felt like they'd been replaced by warm jelly. He held himself up by stepping back and catching himself against the bed.

Bev rolled over sleepily, gazing up at Louis's back. She started to say, "Thank you, honey," at the same time that the light clicked back on.

It took a moment to register. Then she was bolt upright in the bed, eyes wide, and taking a deep breath, which she held ferociously. Louis heard her distress and turned, holding a finger to his lips in a shushing motion. Bev nodded vigorously, her eyes so wide they seemed to glow in the faint light.

"There's someone in the house, Louis!" she whispered in a panicked tone. "Someone's in our house!"

"I know!" Louis whispered back. "We have to do something!"

"We'll call the police. This is their job!" Bev whispered.

"The phones are in the kitchen, charging, remember?"

"Oh 'h'-'e'- double hockey sticks. Louis, what are we going to do?"

The light clicked off, and the house was once again plunged into darkness. Louis bit the inside of his cheek as he thought about the layout of the house.

It was a tri-level floor plan, with the upper floor sitting perpendicular to the main floor. A short hallway to the guest bedroom, with the single bathroom in between. Opposite the bathroom were the stairs down to the living room. A second stairs went down to the garden-level basement. Their daughter Casey was using it for storage as she looked for work after college. All of her things, he remembered, were in boxes in the small room scattered randomly about the floor.

In the center of the living room wall was a fireplace. The backside being part of the kitchen wall. Both he and Bev had spent many a winter day snuggled on the couch under the big bay window, watching the fire crackle merrily.

Louis tried to picture the tree. It was in the living room on the main floor, and should be close to the doorway, which was just beyond the stairs going to the garden floor. It'd be right next to the couch, so it wouldn't help them trying to sneak past the intruder to get to the phones. In fact, he glumly noted, there wasn't any way that a thief wouldn't see them once they got to the bottom of the stairs.

They could, alternately, try to sneak down to the basement and hide in the back room, hoping the thief would leave them alone and be satisfied with taking their jewelry and Louis's cash he kept in a sock in the dresser. Louis didn't think that was going to happen.

*If you're in a house, you're after everything you can get your hands on.*

"Louis? Louis?"

Bev tugged on his sleeve with a strength that nearly pulled him over backwards on the bed. Her lips were right against his ear as she whispered so loudly that Louis was afraid the intruder would hear her too.

"Louis, do you think he's after Casey's boxes?"

Louis thought for a moment. "No, I think he's here for the Christmas presents." He chuckled ruefully, which earned him a hard shake from Bev.

"Louis, we can't let him take any of the presents. Those are for Casey, and y—" Bev clamped her lips shut suddenly.

Beverly thought of the new pocket watch she'd gotten for Louis. His grandfather's watch had been stolen out of his pocket one day at the mall. It'd been done so swiftly that it hadn't registered that someone had taken it for a whole thirty seconds, which by then the thief had already disappeared into the teeming crowd. She knew he'd been heartbroken by the theft, and promised herself she'd find one like it. She had, and scrimped and saved to pay for the watch.

Louis got the same idea that Bev did almost at the same time.

*Casey's gifts are down there too. I finally managed to save enough to get her that little ruby pendant she drooled over at the jeweler's back in April.*

The light clicked back on, faintly illuminating the stairs and the steel blue carpet. Louis' heart sank.

*There's no way we're going to sneak past this guy with the lights on. We have to stay put.*

Bev released her tight grip on Louis, and slowly moved to the opposite side of the bed. To Louis, it felt like she flowed off the bed like a thick syrup, noiselessly lowering her feet to the floor, then moving in a slow crouch to the closet door.

*The closet! They could hide in there until the thief left!*

Louis slowly snuck around the edge of the bed over to Bev, who was slowly grabbing the door handle, and twisting it as quietly as she could. The door protested quietly with a small squeak that froze both of them in place, wincing as if the sound was fingernails scraping across a slate chalkboard.

"Geez, can that be any louder, Bev? That nearly gave me a heart attack," Louis whispered harshly, then shut his mouth and looked back towards the open door.

*I ought to go shut it, that will give us a little warning.*

Louis got two steps towards the door when the lights went out again.

*Oh geez, he heard us!*

Louis froze, then tiptoed back to Bev as she slid inside the closet and then bent over and started rummaging swiftly, and almost quietly, through the loads of sports gear, clothing, and random boxes stashed throughout it.

"Bev, keep it down. He'll hear us."

Bev stopped, and both of them strained to listen in the dark.

The moon had finally emerged from behind the cloud cover and shone through the Venetian blinds over the window, faintly illuminating the room just enough to allow them to make out the dresser, bed, chair, floor lamp, and jacket tree.

Bev returned to slowly rummaging through the clothing and boxes, apparently trying to find something.

A few thumps and bumps later, with Louis cringing with each sound, find something she did, and pulled an aluminum softball bat from the back of the walk-in closet. Bev hefted it and Louis saw her shadowy profile turn to face the door.

Louis was aghast. *Is she intending on taking the guy on herself?! What if he's got a gun?*

The thought had him grabbing at the bat, trying to pull it away from a surprised Bev.

"Louis!" she whispered loudly, "What are you doing!?"

"Let go, Bev. What are YOU doing?!" Louis's harsh whisper was louder than Bev's.

"I'm gonna clobber him upside the head with 'Sweetie'. He doesn't belong in our house."

"Are you bugnuts?! What if he's gotta gun? A baseball bat to a gunfight's a really bad idea."

The two of them struggled for the bat in the closet, and Louis finally pulled it loose from Bev's fierce grip. She pouted sullenly, then suddenly stared past Louis, her eyes going wide. A chill ran up Louis' spine and he spun, nearly smacking Bev in the head as he turned towards the closet doorway.

The light had come back on!

Louis froze again, straining to hear any noise of approaching footfalls.

The light went out.

*What is with this guy? That's three times the damn light's been flipped. Is he jerking us around because he's got no gun? What am I missing?*

Louis was convinced that something was up. Maybe the guy was trying to find them by fiddling with the light to make them come down to check it out.

*Can't be. He's got to have heard us. He screwing with us to keep us up here, because he's got no gun! Wait. Am I fooling myself? What if he does, and this is all a trap!?*

Louis kept going back and forth over the reason for the lights in his mind, then Beth surged past him, ripping the bat from his hands.

She screamed bloody murder as she charged down the steps, with Louis in hot pursuit.

"OH GOD BEV! DON'T! STOP! He'll kill us!"

Louis, in desperation, launched himself from the bottom step and tackled Bev to the ground. She shrieked and conked Louis on the head with the bat, then surged to her feet, ready to do battle with the intruder.

Louis woozily lay on top of Bev. He grabbed drunkenly at her, trying to get between her and the intruder. He had a hazy idea that he should drag her back upstairs, but that all stopped when the tree lights clicked on.

They both yelled in surprise and terror ... and were answered by a strange noise. Bev, fueled by fear of the intruder, rage at their home being invaded, and adrenalin, surged up, bat in hand, lifting Louis with her like he was a dust cloth. Louis hung on for dear life as Bev whirled in a circle looking for the intruder. They both froze as sudden noises came from near the tree.

"Dook! Mrrrrmmmrrrrmrrrmmmm! Dook! Dook! Dook! Dook!"

Louis looked over at the tree. No intruder. No open door or broken glass. The Christmas tree stood tall and perfect. The presents were still under it, especially the all-important present for Bev. The couch and rocking chair were untouched, and nothing torn or broken was on the floor.

Bev shrieked suddenly, drawing his attention. Louis glanced at Bev, who stared wide-eyed at the couch. He turned, ready to fight, and saw a small shape scamper across the couch. It stopped suddenly, and rolled on its back, cradling a smaller, shiny object.

The creature reminded Louis of a tube covered by a fuzzy sock as it lay on the couch, the shiny object held against its belly. Louis recognized the object: a light switch — the switch that Louis had set on the end of a cord. The cord ran to the wall socket where the Christmas tree was plugged in.

They both stared open-mouthed at the vision in front of them. The little fuzzy creature pressed the switch against its belly. The switch made a 'click'. The lights turned off, and the fuzzy creature made soft, excited '*dook*'-ing sounds as it ran crazily across the couch.

After a few moments of those antics, it gamboled back to the switch, and pressed it against its belly again. The lights clicked on, and it was off once more making those '*dook*'ing noises and racing excitedly across the couch.

Casey's ferret.

They'd both forgotten the little creature in their panic. Casey had left the ferret with them while she was in Seattle, interviewing for a job. Somehow, the creature had figured out how to get past the lock on her cage, and was now happily playing with the light switch Louis had rigged so he didn't have to bend over to turn the tree off.

Bev stared at the little brown, bandit-masked animal for a minute, then she let her arms fall. She started giggling quietly — which then grew into a full-throated laugh that filled the whole room.

Louis found himself chuckling with her as they watched the ferret flip the switch, tear off around the couch, and then come back to attack the switch and flip it again. They looked at the tree, the presents, and the ferret.

Finally, they looked at each other and smiled, tears rolling from their eyes.

"Merry Christmas, honey," Louis managed to say through his laughter.

Bev smiled and hugged him. "Merry Christmas to you too, Lou."

"Dook! Dook! Mmmmrrrmmrrm."

... *click!*

# ABOUT THE AUTHOR

J Dark is a latecomer to the writing profession, but enjoying every moment that life will allow. "The best thing to me is writing a story that someone enjoys. If I've made something fun and entertaining for people, it's a win-win."

J Dark lives with a house full of dreams, three cats, and various friends who occasionally drop by and stay for a while. J Dark lives in Kansas, where the winds blow all the time, and, if you blink your eyes, the weather changes.

You can find out more about the works and world of J Dark at *The Pandemonium* (thepandemonium.net).

# YOU MIGHT ALSO ENJOY

## Best Intentions

Book One of the Glass Bottles Series

by J Dark

*When your past is left undone, it will come find you.*

## Broken Bridge

Book Two of the Glass Bottles Series

by J Dark

*Sometimes a broken bridge has to be crossed.*

## Beguiling Voices

Book Three of the Glass Bottles Series

by J Dark

*Never trust magic … or the people that hire you.*

Available from Paper Angel Press in
hardcover, trade paperback, digital, and audio editions
*paperangelpress.com*